W9-DDI-491

PRAISE FOR

"Prendergast's unrhymed verse not only tells the tale, but varies form and line length, the clipped rhythms capturing Ella's emotional turmoil...Sensitive and compelling."

—*Kirkus Reviews*

"A quick read, thanks to the format and the dramatic plot... [Prendergast's] candid approach to sex, lies, and friendship should attract a wide audience."

—*School Library Journal*

"Ella's responses are generally thoughtful and consistently authentic. I like that Ella stands firm in her individuality and owns both her vulnerability and her nonconformity."

—*Resource Links*

"Prendergast is able to portray complete characters, an intricate plot and a variety of settings with a minimum of words... Highly Recommended."

—*CM Magazine*

"Bitterly real, Ella's bad choices and low self-esteem haunt her as she spirals through life...Prendergast is extraordinary."

—*On Page 394* blog

GABRIELLE PRENDERGAST

ORCA BOOK PUBLISHERS

Library and Archives Canada Cataloguing in Publication

Prendergast, Gabrielle, author
Capricious / Gabrielle Prendergast.

Originally published: Victoria, BC, Canada : Orca Book Publishers, ©2014.

Issued in print and electronic formats.
ISBN 978-1-4598-1428-8 (paperback).—ISBN 978-1-4598-0268-1 (pdf).—
ISBN 978-1-4598-0269-8 (epub)

1. Novels in verse. I. Title.
PS8631.R448C36.2017   jc813'.6   C2016-904461-0

First published in the United States, 2014
Library of Congress Control Number: 2016949038

Summary: In this verse novel for teens, Ella's plan to have two secret boyfriends backfires.

RECYCLED
Paper made from
recycled material
FSC
www.fsc.org   FSC® C103567

Orca Book Publishers is dedicated to preserving the environment and has printed this book on Forest Stewardship Council® certified paper.

Orca Book Publishers gratefully acknowledges the support for its publishing programs provided by the following agencies: the Government of Canada through the Canada Book Fund and the Canada Council for the Arts, and the Province of British Columbia through the BC Arts Council and the Book Publishing Tax Credit.

Cover design by Chantal Gabriell and Teresa Bubela
Cover artwork by Janice Kun
Author photo by Leonard Layton

ORCA BOOK PUBLISHERS
www.orcabook.com

Printed and bound in Canada.

20 19 18 17 • 4 3 2 1

For Margaret

chapter one

AUTOMATIC TRANSMISSION

I've never been a girl to make plans
Beyond about a week in advance
Some girls have their whole lives
Laid out like a spreadsheet

Instead I lay myself out
Samir's fingers tracing
The curve of my naked hip
On a blood-spotted white sheet

Are you okay? he says, wide-eyed
Neither of us expected our reunion
To find us tearing at each other's clothes
In the narrow staircase.

He rested his hand on my thigh
As he drove us home from school
And I slid his fingers up and up until
His face flushed hot.

We kissed at the mudroom door and fell inside
Latching the lock behind us

Tumbling upward with arms and legs
And lips and tongues entwined.

It was unplanned and unprepared for.
And Samir is surprised by the blood
I thought you and David might have...
I told you we're just friends, I say.

Though in my mind David flickers
Brightly and briefly.
The half-naked boy next to me
Is enough distraction.

We should have used a condom, Samir says
Grave and shamed
Are you on the pill?
I reassure him: the wrong time of month etc.

Though worry niggles at me
I'll deal with it tomorrow
I know where the clinic is
Every smart girl does.

Samir curls his arm around me
And pulls me close
I've missed you so much, habibti
He says, *I love you.*

Can we be back together?
Can it be like it was?
We won't do this again if you don't want.
We can pretend it never happened.

I stroke his nascent beard
Breathing in his sweaty sweetness
And touch him, everywhere
Claiming all of him back to me.

HIS PRESENCE

Makes my heart
Grow
Fonder
Stronger
Less inclined to
Wander.

Makes me wonder
At my plan
To pretend
That David is
"Just a friend."
To play it out
This selfish drama
All the way
To the end.

MOTHER OF THE YEAR

Mom comes home with groceries
Samir and I are on the couch
The TV on, feet touching
Like nothing special happened.
Samir helps her bring the bags in
It's nice to see you again, Mom says
Will we be seeing more of you?
I hope so, Samir says
And blushes so hard
It makes my heart ache.

When he leaves
I chop carrots and onions
And Mom fixes me in her stare
Until I feel I might crack
And crumble
My skin peeling off in strips
Like old paint.
Do we need to have "the talk"? she says.
Boys look a certain way
When certain things happen
I haven't forgotten.
Your father still gets that look.

Ew, I say.
I suppose you're done with David then?
I want to ask her
What she thinks

If I can have them both
But I know she'll disapprove.
I'm just trying to be mature about it, I say instead
I'm friends with both of them
Nothing happened with Samir.
He's just happy we're talking again
And so am I.

LET'S REVIEW

There are rules
To being a white
Middle-class
Christian (sort of)
Teenage girl:
    1.Be obsessed with clothes
    (I'm not, apart from that one dress)
    2.Have a circle of BFFs
    (HA! My collection of friends is more like a black hole)
    3.Have at most ONE boyfriend
    (Who's counting?)
And some other things
NOT to do

DON'T take naked pictures of yourself
EVER
Just don't do it

DON'T have sex without protection
EVER
Because that's just stupid

DON'T lie to your parents
EVER
That always ends badly

DON'T take drugs

This last at least
I have under control
So far.

BUT THESE ARE MY RULES:

On Clothes:

Maybe I AM obsessed
But it's with the wrong clothes
Or the right ones
Depending on how you look at it.
Because girls' clothes
Speak loudly
She's a slut
She's square
She's a stoner
A nerd
An emo goth
A Muslim
A Mormon
A Jew
So loudly
We sometimes can't hear
Our own voices.
But I don't mind if my clothes speak for me
Though I prefer them to say
She's crazy
After all, it's better
If everyone knows in advance.

On BFFs and Black Holes:

One girlfriend might be manageable
But they travel in pairs
Or packs
And their density
Stretches me thin
Gravity sucking me
Down
Into the dark places
That are next to
Impossible
To escape.

On Boys:

I'm sixteen years old
Not sixty
Not old and bored
And married.
Are you guys together?
Are you, like, a couple?
What does that even mean?
Do the things I've done with Samir
Mean he owns me?
And the things I haven't done with David
Mean he doesn't?
What if I
Want to own
Them
Both?

LOGISTICS

There are details
That need working out
Some chess pieces that need
To be carefully placed.

But for now

I swish the spotted sheets from the bed
And bleach them
With my gym socks
And white cotton nightgown.

I watch a movie

With Kayli wheezing behind the nebulizer mask
She's sticking with homeschooling until June
Mom enjoys teaching her, I think
And she's learning stuff she never thought she would.

I watch Mom

Make dinner and eat dinner
And help her tidy up
And follow her around for an hour
Until I'm sure she won't barf.

I wait for Dad

He comes home with a pile of essays
And groans as he reads them
Undergrads, he says, despairing
Confusing Constantine and Commodus.

Those morons, I say

Knowing I could never keep my emperors straight
They're all penguins to me
But the past has always confused me
I can barely manage the present.

FRESH SHEETS

I run my hand over the place
Where Samir lay
Wide-eyed
Breathless
I lied when he asked
Did I hurt you?

I want to hold that moment

They say you never forget
Your first
And I'm not likely to
But just to be sure
I pull out my sketchpad and pencils
And try to find the right
Lines and curves
The way the afternoon light
Dappled the sheets.

But I get stuck on his hand
Holding my face
As he kissed me
Like he thought
I might turn away.

Disembodied
I pin the hand above the bed

And watch it hover over me
Protectively
Possessively
Most of the night.

ANXIETY

I dream of condoms
And lies
And David

And wake up thinking
I am under arrest again.

GOOD FRIDAY

Mom makes fish and chips
Which we eat in front of the TV
Watching *Jesus Christ Superstar*
While I count the hours
Twenty-four, twenty-five
Twenty-six, twenty-seven
Since Samir and I
Did not use a condom.

The clinic is closed today
In honor of the Crucifixion
Of our Savior.
There is irony in there
Somewhere
But I can't be bothered
To winkle it out.

Instead
I smother my anxiety
In vinegary chips
And sneak a beer
It's half-drunk before Dad notices
And scowls at me.

Technically, I know,
I have seventy-two hours
But each hour that clicks by
I worry and wonder
If I've stupidly succumbed to
The mother of all screwups.

HOLIDAY HOURS

Women's clinics should be like peep shows
With discreet private booths.

Instead I transgress a line of protestors
Who should be getting ready for Easter
If they're as Christian as they claim.
I give the finger to each and every one
And wait with weeping girls
Churlish, chastened boys
And a few disappointed mothers
To speak to a nurse counselor
About morning-afters.

You might have some cramping, she says
And gives me a box of condoms
For *next time*
Before running through some thought-provoking
questions
Are you safe at home?
Are you safe with your boyfriend?

Yes, I say
I would love to explain to her
That I felt so safe with Samir in my bed
That I never wanted to leave.
I wanted to pull the sheet over our heads
And cocoon us in that soft cotton world.

At the thought
My eyes fill with tears
Happy ones
But who can tell the difference?
So she says,
Is there anything else you want to talk about?

MY LIFE

Yes, my life
I say
As if that provides adequate parameters
For the rest of my fifteen minutes.

The nurse only nods
Her pencil poised to record
Anything pertinent.

I only moved here last year, I say
And I went to a new school
And I thought things might be different
Better, but in fact
They were much, much worse.

I met this boy, Samir
And he was so special
And so right for me
And wrong
That my brain kind of frazzled
And thought it would be a good idea
To take a picture of my pussy
And turn it into art
To display at school.

I pause there
Giving the poor woman time
To write something down.
I heard of this case, she says

That was you?
You were arrested, right?

I nod
And take a deep breath
Because I feel a little faint
Like my history is blood
And I'm pouring it onto the floor.

Another boy
David is his name
He put the picture on Facebook
And sent it to a younger friend
Who is a MORMON for God's sake
And would you believe
He wants to date my sister?
Anyway, his parents weren't impressed
Or people you want to trifle with.
I breathe again
I breathe
The threads of David and Samir
Tangling and untangling in my mind.

So that was bad enough, I go on
Then this girl, Genie
Took against me
I think she was jealous
Of the attention I was getting

Kids started writing on this wall
Messages of support and unity
I think I became kind of a folk hero
For about five minutes.

But Genie also had a thing for Samir
So she framed him
For a hate crime
And he was going to get arrested too
And everything I tried to do
To fix it
Only made it worse
So we thought we'd run away
But his father caught us together
And even though he was
Surprisingly understanding
I screwed it up again
And ran off
Because something came back
From my old life
And blew me to pieces.

I wait
Breathing
Blinking the stars from my eyes
I see, the nurse says
And what was that?

DARKNESS

I feel sorry for her
Because I know she's imagining the worst
Some boy mashing me down
Behind a car
Outside a party
That kind of thing.

But before I open my mouth
And tell her what really happened
I remember only four people know
Mom, Dad, Kayli
And Samir, kind of.
I haven't even told David.

So instead I say
    My baby brother died
    When I was nine
The half-lie slips out
Slippery as a newborn seal
    It upsets me sometimes.

Upsets you?
She consults her notes
"Blew me to pieces," you said
That sounds like a bit more than upset
Can you tell me more?
How did he die?

It's easy enough to cry
Over the brother I never had
I only ever saw a photo
Of his tiny unfinished feet
My tears seem to satisfy her
So I don't explain.

There are only two women
I trust in the whole world
And she's not one of them.

TWO WOMEN

Mom
Because she bore me
She has to love me.

And Kayli
Because in the end
She needs me
As much as
I need her.

BUT BOYS ON THE OTHER HAND

Sometimes I think of David
With his cell phone
Snickering as he took a picture
And sent it to his friends.

I don't like the memory
It seemed so unlike him
The considerate boy
I know now.
What did he think
At that moment?
Did he think my art was a joke?

He apologizes repeatedly
For the catastrophe he unleashed on me
Until his remorse gets tiresome
But still I wonder at the impulse
That made him do it.

Like the impulse that Samir got
To reject me and take me back
Deactivate and reactivate our love
Like an email account.

I've told them I forgive them
And I think I do
But maybe that's just
A misguided impulse too.

MORE QUESTIONS

David asks
Are you ready?
I mean, are you sure?

He's worried about me because
He knows school is hard to endure.

And Mom says
We could finish the year at home
You'll pass your exams easily

She's worried about me because
She understands fragility.

And Kayli says
Try not to get arrested
Or cause another revolution

She's worried about me because
She's seen my trails of destruction.

And Dad says
Get on the bus and come to my office
Anytime you can't manage

He's worried about me because
He's the one who pays for the damage.

And I say to myself
Get it together this time, for real
High school is not brain surgery

I'm not worried because
Well...not really.

(SECOND) FIRST DAY OF SCHOOL

I text Samir first thing
Public or private?
And get the answer I expect.
Private, he texts
Because someone will blab
And
We'll
Be
Back
Where
We
Started.

Both God and Allah know
No one wants to be there.
And I too would rather avoid
The judgment
The gossip
The assumptions
The jealousy
And all the other
Bullshit
That high school
L.O.V.E.
Involves.

But still
It sucks that

Of all the things
Samir feels
For me
One
Has to be

Shame.

THE FREEDOM WALL

I find it
The Freedom Wall
Where my classmates
Recorded their outrage
The black scribbles have expanded
To cover the whole wall
A bucket of felt pens
Invites me to add my mark.
The school endorses the Freedom Wall now
With reservations:
No Swearing, a small sign says
Someone has commented *fuck that*
My body, my decision
Someone wrote *Ella Rocks*
And someone else, *Ella Sux*
And a third, *Who is Ella?*
Good question.
She's a bitch and a slut,
Someone answers
Helpfully.
Pretty sure I know
Who wrote that.
As for me
I barely remember being Ella
Barely remember anything
Before I was arrested
And charged
And acquitted for making pornography

Before my life fell apart
Before a piece of art
Reversed my
Rebirth and
Redefined me
Again
As Raphaelle.

THE CENTER PANEL

I still have it
That offending
Offensive
Photograph
Of the most
Intimate
Part
Of me.

I still love it
Like a Georgia O'Keeffe
Pink orchid petals
Hidden
In the back of my closet.

I still think
It's the best thing
I've ever done
And it was all worth it
Because of the Freedom Wall
Because of Samir
Because of David

None of that
Would have happened
If it wasn't for that little word
That starts with C.

Now I add
A curly Celtic *C*
In the top left corner
Of the Freedom Wall
A bold varsity *U*
In the top right
A scrolled *N*
In the bottom left
A *T* like a crucifix
In the bottom right.
I don't sign my name

I'm wicked
Not stupid.

PRINCIPLES AND PRINCIPALS

I get called to the principal's office
Before the first bell even rings
And have to check the mental record
Of my recent history
Wondering if anything I've done
Warrants another expulsion.

My cornerstone embellishments
To the Freedom Wall?

My deflowering
Of a devout Muslim
On the mudroom stairs?

I would love to tell
Principal Pinch Face
The depths of my depravity
But he begins with a peace offering
Such as it is.

I'd like us to start fresh, he says
*As though you're just new at this school
And I know nothing of your record.*

My "permanent record"
I try not to smirk
Maybe the threats are all true.
Maybe that will never leave me.

Scarlet letters
AGITATOR stamped on my forehead.

Traditionally, he continues
The seniors plan a winter trip
This coming winter is New York.
We fundraise for about half the cost
And students contribute the rest
About a thousand dollars each.

It's his turn to smirk
As if saying
I dare you.

ONE THOUSAND DOLLARS

My parents could probably afford it.
But Pinch Face knows I'm proud
And knows there's 15 percent unemployment
In this college town
And knows how "difficult" I am
And that everyone knows it.
He has just done that thing
That bad teachers do
When they make it clear
They think you'll amount to nothing
But trouble.

I could tell him
To take his New York trip
And shove it up his ass
Because it will just be
A bunch of high-school kids
Taking tours and shopping.

On the other hand
I'm pretty sure
There's something
Greater
Waiting for me
In New York.

WORK

I try to imagine
What kind of job
I could do
What kind of employer
Would tolerate me.

I try to picture myself
In a blue fast-food uniform
Or Walmart smock
Or mowing lawns
Or bussing tables.

I try to think
Of a way
To earn a thousand dollars
Without breaking laws
Or losing my mind.

I try to steel myself
For the tedium
The pedantic boss
The dull-witted co-workers
The canned music.

I try to swallow
The humiliating thought
That one day
No matter how hard I try
I'll probably turn into my mother.

THE PRODIGAL DAUGHTER

In happier moments
I imagined my return to school
Like the end of a movie.
I imagined crowds of new friends
Drawn to me by notoriety
Wanting part of my famous wall
United in scorn against convention
Expectation and judgment.

I imagined the ones who sided with me
Gathering around cheering
Slapping me on the back
Maybe even laying palm fronds at my feet.

I imagined I would slip back into school
And find it finally fit me
Comfortable as a pair of worn pajamas
But more flattering.

In happier moments
I imagined a circle of girlfriends
Who didn't make me
Hyperventilate.

In darker moments
I pictured slinking in
Past the smokers
The gossiping girls

The leering boys
Nose pinched against
The faint smell
Of failure and fear
Largely invisible
To a world where my existence
Was still mostly irrelevant.

Take a guess which
Possibility
Came true.

CLASSMATE

David eats his lunch with me
Thank God
Because I'm not sure anyone else
Would be game.

Samir watches warily
But when I catch him staring
He grins
A sly, slow grin.

As the rest of the school
Stumbles around us
Mind-numbed by sugar
And factoids

And desperation
Crawling, clawing
Creeping upward or sliding downward
On the popularity scale.

David eats his lunch with me
Even though he must know
That in my company
The only way is down.

GIRLS

Sarah
Who I called "Puffy Blond"
But only to myself
Whose mom drove me to the hospital
On Christmas Day
And listened when I defended Samir
From a terrible accusation
Sarah, who is probably a nice person
Under it all

Sarah
Ignores me.

Genie
Who was Sarah's best friend
Before she defaced a painting
With unforgivable slurs
And blamed Samir
She is a vengeful manipulator
Not to be trusted

Genie
Has amassed a new entourage.

Sarah and Genie
Have divvied up our year
Into two lip-glossed militias
Hair-sprayed armies

Who occupy the halls
In a fragile cold war
And they all blame me.

Me
Who eschews the politics
Of girlhood
I tiptoe around them
Avoiding their minefields
And roadside bombs
I'm a pacifist
And a bit of a coward

I
Would rather not take sides.

ESSAY DRILL

It's the usual waste of time
The usual crime of taking teenage brains
And putting them in chains
We should be in our creative prime
Instead we're dwindling and unwinding
Grinding our ideas into fine dust
Letting them rust in five neat piles
With encouraging smiles
You keep telling us we must
Think of college, sink all our knowledge
Into this one stupid essay, *S-A*
S-A-T, are you satisfied?
Half my classmates have anxiety
Or are stupefied by pharmaceuticals
Or destined for cubicles

It is often said that our struggles teach us the most
Discuss.

If this were true, half the kids here
Would be geniuses
Because in this bubble they struggle
With every trouble the other kids have
Only double
Can't read, can't write
Can't avoid a fight
And then there are kids who can't walk

Or talk
Can't dress themselves, not even a sock
Kids who drink, who can't think
Forget about swimming; with them
It's sink or sink.

PERSPECTIVE

I know it's wrong
To think of Marika this way
Ms. Sagal's silent daughter
Her odd contorted posture
Frail, unpredictable arms.
I know the photo I took of her
Last year, *Disabled*
Was supposed to be ironic.
Because one word
Could never sum her up.
Her laugh is infectious
Her silence is mesmerizing
Her art blows my mind.
Wild swirls and fractured words
Like Basquiat.

The other girls look at her
With mournful eyes
And patronizing smiles.
She smiles back
The multitudes of Marika
But once, I'm pretty sure
She winked at me.

Sometimes I think
I should have her problems
Her "struggles"
Could teach me a thing or two.

DAD

Dad asks me
Predictably
How was your first day?

One-syllable answers
Should be enough.

Fine, I say
Chill
Dull.

The multi-syllables
Terrifying
Solitary
Meaningless
Discouraging
Soul destroying
No different
From last year.
A hotbed of
Temptation
Irritation
Oppression
Subjugation
Perplexity
And despair
I keep to myself.

chapter two

RAIN

Wet snow turns to rain
Melts the white icing away
Revealing gray roads.

This spring, so unlike
The frayed-edge coastal seasons,
Is bold, harsh and quick.

I never thought it
Possible that I'd ever
Grow to love winter.

But spring here explodes
With gleeful celebration
Green, fresh and fertile.

RELIEF

Speaking of fertility
My body gives me a break for once.
My period started,
I whisper to Samir
Before art class.
Alhamdulillah, he replies
Eyes turned upward
And we both laugh at the irony.

What's so funny?
David says
Trailing into class after us.
Your haircut, Samir says.
I frown at him
But David just shakes his head
Fake laughing.
Hilarious, Sam, he says
You should have a TV show.

And Samir flips him off
Then makes a game
Of picking invisible bugs
From my hair
As an excuse to touch me
Until David says
Why don't you get some manners?
And Samir says
Why don't you get a personality?

And I say
Why don't you both
Just get your dicks out
And measure them?
Only I say it so loud
The whole class hears.

And Genie says
Are you planning another artwork?
Penises this time?
And Ms. Sagal frowns
Before gently reminding us
The phallus is a popular theme
In modern art
But for now
Let's keep it PG.

INK

Ink
Black lines
The shape of
David's hand
Strong
And open
Like a bed
I could curl into
His fingers
Soft
And safe
His hand stained
With black
Ink.

PROCRASTINATION

The truth is
Samir and I
Have gone through that box of condoms
Since the incident on the stairs
And I'm still no closer
To altering David's friendship
Into something more.

The truth is
I'm
Afraid
Of
Losing
Him.

The truth is
When I say
"Losing him"
I'm not sure
Which "him"
I mean.

The truth is
Part of me
Wants to run away
From both of them
Before they can
Hurt me again.

The truth is
In the dark
Of my room
Their outlined hands
Pinned to my wall
Look like claws.

The truth is
What I say
About not wanting
To be normal
Is not actually
The truth.

SPRING FLING

Kayli twirls
In the vintage pink chiffon dress
It's a twirlish dress, she says
Tugging at the high neck.

Don't twirl too much, I say
Or the boys will see your underwear.
You'd know, Kayli quips
And twirls so fast
The dress flies up
And gives me an eyeful
Of plain white cotton panties.

Like them?
She asks, pursing her lips.
I picked them in his honor.
She's referring to her Mormon date.
A solemn fourteen-year-old
Who waits upstairs with David.

You need a better bra
She says, eyeing my insufficient chest
In the green V-necked bodice.
Try this one.
I slip the dress down
And hook the new bra in place
While Kayli manhandles my boobs
Like uncooperative children.

Turn, she commands
And the two ripe, round
Creamy buns spilling from the dress
Nearly blind me.
That, my baby sister says
Is why they call it WonderBra.

EYE CONTACT

Poor David
He really tries

To look me in the eyes

Go ahead
Take a good look, it's okay

Let's just get it out of the way.

Wow, he says to my cleavage
Blushing red as a stop sign

You look divine.

His smile
Sheepish, disarming

Is utterly charming.

DOUBLE DATE

Kayli's date, Parker
Is only allowed "group dates"
And invited me and David along
As a peace offering
After all the fuss last year.

In a quiet moment
While David hangs our coats
And Kayli powders her nose
Parker fidgets and sighs
And finally says, *Sorry.*

Not your fault, I say
Thirteen years old
What were you supposed to do
With a picture like that?
Really, it's David's fault.

You're Catholic, right?
Is that why you forgave him?
David returns from the coat check
Looking splendidly rakish.
One of the reasons, I say.

DAVID

He's one of those handsome boys
Who lurks in the shadow
Of a more handsome brother
Skates across the ice
After a better sniper
Struggles through classes
That his brother aced.

He's one of those sweet boys
You would think
Had a new girl each week
But as he confessed to me
Has had no girls at all
Ever.

He's one of those happy boys
Whose laughter hides
A darker side
A deeper struggle
A brain that buzzes
A heart that longs
For praise he never gets.

He's one of those lost boys
Just waiting
To be found
I guess that's how
He ended up
With me.

SLOW DANCING

Eyes turn
And whispers hiss
David and ELLA?

My head rests
Cheek to his chest
Ella and DAVID?

His fingers tiptoe
Around my hip
David and ME.

LITTLE BLACK DRESSES

Genie and her clique
Corner me in the ladies room
Like crows converging on carrion.

Pretty dress, Ella, Genie says
But what on EARTH is your sister wearing?
Her friends cackle on cue.

It's vintage, I say, but your dresses are lovely.
Was it one respectable dress
That you cut into three?

They giggle, like I've just complimented them
For showing so much skin
And their legs, backs and boobs slink out.

Leaving me, heart galloping
My fingers curled around the sink
So tight it hurts.

FIRST KISS

Have you seen Kayli?
I ask David
Worried now that Genie will
Go after her too.

I'm feeling
The gloss wearing off
The sparkle dimming
The champagne bubbles popping
On Spring Fling.

Now I just
Want to
Go
Home.

We find Kayli and Parker
By the fountain
Her pressed against
A Grecian column.

The hem of the pink dress
Is bunched in Parker's fist
On her thigh.
Are you all right?
David asks her.

My sister.
My fourteen-year-old
Baby
Sister.

She grins
Lipstick smeared
Starry eyed.
I'm great,
She says
And you?

DRIVEWAY

We drop off Parker first
OUT, David says
As Kayli's goodnight kiss
Gets slightly out of hand.

Later, Kayli runs barefoot
Up our driveway
I see her barreling down the hall
As the front door swings closed.

She'll be calling all her girlfriends,
I tell David, to give them a report.
What about you? he asks
Will you be reporting to your girlfriends?

I could say, "What girlfriends?"
Or "What's to report?"
But instead I look at my knees
While David loosens his tie.

TRANSITION

Did you have fun?
Yes. Did you?
Yes. Would you like to go out with me again?
We go out together all the time.
We saw *Cats* last week.
Right. Singing cats.
That was brilliant.
Better than that so-called hockey game.
No, no, that was wrestling.
Ice wrestling?
Yes. That's a thing now.
Didn't you know?
You're cute when you snort.
You look good in a suit.
Right?
I might wear it to school.
Can you imagine?
Parker is not a very good Mormon, is he?
You're not a very good Catholic.
You're not a very good Jew.
What do you mean?
I'm circumcised!
Ew. TMI.
You ate five pounds of pork ribs
Right in front of me.
Those were emu ribs.
Emu?
Possibly ostrich. Or wombat.

It was Friday night
And you drove.
You're right.
I'm a terrible Jew.
I'm not smart enough to start with
And I'm too tall.
Oh, they have tall Jews now.
They do?
Yes, it's new.
Who are "they" exactly?
Sears.
I see.
In the racial-stereotype department?
Yes. It's right next to lingerie.
I love it when girls say "lingerie."
Even the word is sexy.
It's hilarious when boys say it.
Say "mascara."
Mascara.
You're snorting again.
I can't help it.
You're funny.
That's because I'm Canadian.
Stop snorting!
Are you making me laugh
So my boobs will jiggle?
What?! No!
But awesome idea.

I haven't even been looking.

That's because you're a gentleman.

No, it's also because I'm Canadian.

You're right.

They ARE jiggling.

David!

What?

It was your idea.

They're like milky Jell-O balls.

That's the worst boob metaphor
I've ever heard.

Surely not.

How many have you heard?

And wasn't that a simile?

Thank you, Captain Language Arts.

YOU snorted!

I did not.

That was a chortle.

I should get inside.

I'll walk you to the door.

TEXT

There's a beep
An odd chirp
From David's pocket
And everything changes.

His smile becomes
A frown.
His laughter becomes
Silence.

His offer to walk me to the door
Vanishes.

His phone appears
And our joy
Our fun night out
Ends somehow.

What is it?
What's the matter?
Are you okay?

Fine, he says
But I have to go.

SILENCE

The house feels empty
Though it's only sleeping.

My head feels heavy
Though it's also churning.

David's car peels away into the dark
But curiosity stays with me.

It's not my business.
He's not my boyfriend.

I'm slightly whiplashed though
By his change of mood.

For all Samir's complexity
David is even harder to read.

DARKNESS: PART TWO

I'm thinking of u,
Samir texts.

At this time of night
This is cheeky code
For something
Rather crude
And according to his beliefs
Forbidden.

Me 2,
I text back.
Not quite true
But close enough.

AFTERGLOW

Sent an email, he texts.

I read it
Phone light
Glowing bluish
Around me.

Last time
Before I broke up with you
I was always so happy
When we were together
But miserable
Full of doubt
And guilt
When we were apart.

This time
Happiness lingers
Erasing
The misery
And doubt
And guilt
Day and night
Every minute
I'm blissfully
In love
With you.

XO,
Your Samir

NIGHT LIGHT

A dream
A coyote's howl
Launches me
Into the dark
Real world
As mystery trips away
Like a tail flicking
Slipping through
Grasping fingers
Momentarily
I wonder
If it isn't
Really

                  Me

I'm afraid
Of

                              Losing.

PINK MARKER

In predawn lamplight
I scribble out Parker's hand
His trimmed fingernails
And boring watch
Skinny wrist
His pale, stumpy fingers
Fisting a handful of chiffon
On Kayli's thigh.

I do the whole thing
In nauseating pink ink
A feeble attempt
To emasculate him
For touching my sister.

OUT OF SYNC

The bell rings
The crowd parts
Like a salty sea
I drift from class
To class
A watery
Washed-up
Ghost.

The teachers start
Looking through me
As though I'm glass
Or falling ash
Like something
Scraped off
Toast.

My classmates see
A repentant smart-ass
I never asked
Who my prank
Would hurt
Most.

Unmasked
At last

I let them
Gloat.

They pass
A note.

INTERCEPTED LIES

She thinks she's so edgy.

She's obsessed with her hoo-hoo.

LOL! Free speech my flappy labia.

Snort! No one even writes on that stupid wall anymore.

It was a boring fad.

They should paint over it.

I heard she practically STALKS David.

He's a loser too. He used to be cool.

He's so MOODY now.

Wouldn't YOU be with a brother like that?

She turned Sam gay.

LOL! You're terrible.

I know.

BOREDOM AND HUMILIATION

After months of homeschooling
Regular school is hard to take
And I have to keep my nose
Squeaky clean.

I'm tempted to enlarge the note
On the library photocopier
And paper the stairwell
And staff lounge.

But Principal Pinch Face
Is just waiting for an excuse.
I don't think he enjoyed
Looking the bad guy last year.

That part at least
Is not my fault.
No one forced him
To suspend me.

He drops hints.
I'm told your sister
Will join us in the fall.
Won't that be nice?

And I hear:
"I hope she's not

As much of a screw-up
As you."

If you want to go on
The New York trip
You will have to join
A fundraising group.

I try not to choke
At this new horror
But before the last bell
Am down for "car wash."

FRIENDSHIP

Samir's arms are crossed
When I get into the car.
I buckle in
And wait
Resisting the urge
To kiss the pout
From his pretty lips.
What's your deal with David?
He asks.
It's not like I haven't been
Expecting this.

What deal? We're friends
I say, looking down
At my dorky skirt
And serious shoes.
He took you to Spring Fling?

I explain the "group date" thing
And try to make him laugh
By telling him it sounds
Kinky to me.

Samir is not quite appeased.
Why do you hang around
With that dumb jock?
I would like to tell him
That David is far from dumb

But that's not really
What this is about.

I'm entitled to friends
I say, and it comes out decisively
More than how it feels.
Because I think I'm rewriting
The book of friendship
And entitlement.

GIRLS

Why can't you be friends with girls?
He asks and forgets to add:
"Like a normal person."

It's almost as though he doesn't know
He's asking for the moon.

I've been "friends" with girls before,
I remind him. How'd that turn out?
Wait. No, I remember. One bunch
Tried to kill me, and last year
My "friend" nearly got you arrested.
So excuse me if I prefer David.
David has no reason to hurt me.
David already feels responsible
For everything that happened
And if David wants something more
He'll tell me and I'll tell you. Okay?
Anyway, if you're ready
To defy your parents and go public
Be my real-life boyfriend again
David will respect that.
Right now he thinks you and I
Are just friends, like you want him to.
So what am I supposed to say?
My "friend" Samir doesn't want to share?

I take a breath
Shocked that all that
Came out of my mouth.
I guess it needed to be said.

Samir is not happy, but behind
Those dark and brooding eyes
Behind that conflict
Is a reasonable boy who loves me
And trusts me too, which maybe
I don't quite deserve.

chapter three

UNEXPECTED

SHOPPING MALL

I rue the day
I vowed
To get a job.
I think I'd really
Rather
Be a slob.
The mall where
I try to sell
My soul
Is so dark
I might become
A hairless mole.

MY RESUME

Ella, short for elephant
Student
Troublemaker
Seducer of pious boys.

Ella, short for Raphaelle
Fallen angel
Artist
Pornographer.

Ella, who hates
Fashion
Fast food
And most people.

Ella, yes, *that* Ella
Yes, I did go to jail
(For one night)
No, I DON'T have a record.

Ella, founder of
The Freedom Wall
Finder of flaws
Photographer.

No, I don't have
Any experience
Or skills
To offer you.

Yes, I
Really
Need
A job.

EXHAUSTION

Mom tries to be encouraging
It took me a long time to find something.
She's now teaching ESL kids
How to read.

I don't have "a long time," I say
Face down on my futon
Smelling Samir on my pillow
Though I don't mention that
To her.

We can pay for the trip
Your father doesn't mind.
No way, I say
I want to do it myself
I've cost you enough this year.

Lawyers and shrinks
Don't come cheap
Though I'm done
With them both
For now.

Kayli needs new medicine
Her asthma's getting worse
And Mom's still in therapy
(Speaking of shrinks)
And Dad's not made of money.

I'll keep looking, I say
I'll find something.
Mom's silence whispers
Her worry
About me.

WORRY

They talk in lowered voices
I hear them in the TV room
They speak of jobs and college choices
Like one misstep could spell my doom.

I hear them in the TV room
The sound is turned low enough
Like one misstep could spell my doom
I'm not so weak that I can't face this stuff.

The sound is turned low enough
Do they want me to know they don't believe
I'm not so weak that I can't face this stuff?
So quiet now that I can barely breathe.

Do they want me to know they don't believe
In me, in my maturity? They talk
So quiet now that I can barely breathe
Through my shame, my hurt, my shock.

They discuss me like I'm a notion
They speak of jobs and college choices
They whisper like the distant ocean
They talk in lowered voices.

ANOTHER TRIP AROUND THE SUN

One year ago
I was planning
And packing
And not worrying
That I had no one to invite
To my sweet sixteen.

Kayli and I
Were Michaela and Raphaelle then.
We "borrowed" a bottle of wine
And drank it out of travel mugs
On the beach
While the sun set
And Kayli complained
About leaving all her friends.

This year
She invites her new friends
To my birthday-party barbecue
And Mom invites her student, Nina
Who is my age and has a baby
And Dad invites some grad students
Who drink imported beer.

And I invite
Samir AND David
Just because I can.

Ignoring each other
They circle me
As seventeen
Begins.

NINA'S SON

I remember
Neglected dolls
Hard, cold plastic

Their chemical smell
Like funeral homes
Or janitors' closets.

So unlike

The baby's soft, fat foot
Cupped in my hand
Warm and smooth

His glossy head
Black and sleek
As an otter.

LAST MAN STANDING

Sam looked like he saw a ghost
David says
When you had Nina's baby in your lap.
He has stayed to help clean up.
Samir has gone to work.
There but for the grace of Allah?
I say.
David stares into the soapy sink
Silent.

I could all-out lie
Tell him Samir and I are through
And that would fit in with my plan
But I'm learning
Lying is not so easy.

At least, not to the boy
Who actually talks to me
At school.

THE SECOND

The moment
We step out the door
Summer arrives.
The earlier rain
Rinsed spring away.

The instant
The wind grows warm
I slip my cardigan off
And fling it
Over a lawn chair.

The moment
I sit on the bottom stair
David sits behind me
And trails his fingers
On my bare shoulders.

The instant
My skin shivers
His sigh tickles my neck.
I turn and kneel
Facing him for

The second
Of
Our
First
Kisses.

DAVID'S DISCLAIMER

I didn't think
You would ever
Let me do that
Again,

He says.

I've been trying
To forget about it
But I really like you.
You've probably noticed.

Say something.

Or not.

LIPS

We kiss for a long time
His hands on my neck
And back.
It's chaste
Innocent
Like after-school-TV
Church-picnic
Prom-picture
Kisses.
I try to invite
More
Parting my lips
Sliding my hands
Around him
And just as I feel
His tongue's
Tentative
Touch
His phone chirps
And our kiss
Dies.

GUILT

I watch him leave
He barely says a word
Nothing to worry about
Then he's gone.

His taillights blink
At the corner
And disappear
In the golden horizon.

My skin tingles
From his fingers
On my collarbone
And the shiver of guilt.

This is what I wanted
What I planned
But the reality
Is something unexpected.

Donning my cardigan
I try to ignore
The sensation
Of tearing in two.

DRY EYES

Last year I cried a lot
Like monsoon season
West Coast winters
Pacific storms.

Last year I flew apart
Like an eagle's nest
Torn from a treetop
Flung into the wind.

Last year I showed the world
My most intimate part
Scaring even myself
With my foolishness.

This year my eyes sting
I blink away
The dry summer dust
And doubts.

This year
I will store
The foul weather
Inside.

ALL A GIRL NEEDS

A summer job
Money
An occupation
A settled family
A soft place to land

An image
Single
Carefree
Cautious
Sensible

A secret
Reckless heart
Two boys
And maybe
Too much love.

chapter four

INSUFFICIENT

MARIKA

I encounter Marika
Ms. Sagal's daughter
At the Apple Store
(They're not hiring).
Are you getting an iPad?
She nods, jerky, wordless.
We want to try the speech apps
Her classroom aide says.
Apparently, they're great.

Marika bends her fingers
And makes a face at me
Smacking a large black box
In her lap.
Your old one hurts your fingers?
I ask.
Her aide grins.
That's very good.
Intuitive.
I shrug.
It seemed pretty obvious.

Some people are intimidated.
Some people are dickheads
I say.

The aide frowns
But Marika laughs
An explosive
Full-body laugh
And presses
One curved hand
To her mouth
Her eyes bright.

Coffee?
I say,
I'd love some.

PATIENCE

Sometimes

I

Sign

Sometimes

I

Use

A

Speech aid.

Sometimes

I

P-R-E-F-E-R

To

Listen.

Sometimes

I

Like

T-O-T-A-L

Silence.

MARIKA'S VOICE

It's not at all robotic
Because it comes with
Sighs and giggles
Or frowning concentration.

With an expectant stare
She demands comment.

I like silence too, I say
And listening.

Good.

Words

Are

P-R-E-C-I-O-U-S.

But

So

Are

J-E-W-E-L-E-D

S-W-O-R-D-S

And

S-I-L-V-E-R

D-A-G-G-E-R-S.

And maybe that's
The most brilliant thing
I've ever heard.

DISTRACTION

Only when I'm waiting for the bus
Do I remember
That I forgot
AGAIN
To apply for any jobs.

DRIVING TEST

It's a rite of passage
Mom says
And Dad says
We've practiced a lot

And both Samir and David
Have let me drive their cars
In parking lots
At night.

I should pass this test.

I mean, how hard can it be?
Total morons drive
I've seen them
Tasteless graceless music
Pumping out their
Glinting tinted windows.

GENIE drives, for god's sake.

But there are things I'm good at:
Art, insults, agitation, sex
(According to Samir).
And things I suck at:
Having normal friends

Wearing normal clothes
Being normal.

And, apparently,
Driving.

CAR WASH

Even though I'd rather not think
About cars for a few days
At least until I can book another test
I have to meet with a dozen giggling girls
To plan the car wash.
Why aren't there any boys here?
I ask, which sets off more giggling
And gasping, girls grabbing each other
And rolling black-ringed eyes.
It's a BIKINI car wash, Ella
Like that should be obvious.

Let's elect a chairwoman
Someone says
Ignoring the obvious signs
That I'm having a heart attack
A stroke or mental breakdown.
Someone nominates Genie
Who didn't giggle or gasp
Or grab anyone
At my faux pas.
She only glared
At me.

A PRIVATE WORD

I know you,
Genie says
I know this is the kind of thing
That you'd love to mess with
I'm sure you'd call it
"Objectification"
Or "degrading."
But we don't care
What you think.
This is a tradition
So let's make a deal.
You sit in meetings
And shut up
And on the day
Turn up in a bikini
Waxed and tanned
Ready to wash cars
Or even better
Go to hell
Right now.

GENIE

It's not exactly my fault she hates me
I didn't know last year
That she had a thing for Samir
He didn't tell me about their history.

And yes, I kind of hacked into her laptop
But that was just for fun at first
And she was the one who framed Samir
For vandalizing Sarah's art.

Yes, technically it's my fault
She was grounded for two months
Because maybe there was another way
To prove Samir's innocence.

Though in my defense I was also
Looking at going to jail or worse
And probably not operating on
Full mental capacity.

And yes, for a while it did look like
I'd stolen her best friend forever
But Sarah and I never really clicked
She hangs out with other Jewish kids now.

And okay, Genie and David used to be friends
But he's over her bad attitude, he says.
So maybe she thinks if I'd never been born
Her life would just be that much better.

SWOON

The only thing
That restores my will
To live in the horrid
Aftermath
Of spending lunch
With twelve girls
Imagining us all
In bikinis
(Waxed and tanned?!)
Covered with foam
And water
Squirming and writhing
Like strippers in training
Is the thought
Of Samir's worship
His awed reverence
His adoration
At the altar
Of me.

Tell me I'm beautiful,

I text him.

He replies in seconds.

Like sunset
And sunrise
And all the stars
In between.

WHERE DO I SIGN?

Marika has been talking about you.
I help her put the ink pots away
Carefully tightening each lid.
I learned THAT the hard way
Ms. Sagal jokes.

Marika doesn't warm up to everyone
She hates to be pitied
Or talked down to.

I'm not sure what to say
I can relate
I hate pity too
And pretention
And patronizing
"When I was your age"
And so on.

Marika's aide usually
Works with her.
They spend the summer
Hanging out.
I teach summer school.

The ink pots are lined up
On the shelf like patient soldiers
Their tin helmets screwed on tight.
Ms. Sagal closes the cupboard
And locks it.

Marika's aide is spending the summer
In Peru
Some sort of language grant
So I was wondering
If you'd like to work with us.

With Marika
All summer
Just hanging out
For money.

IRONIC (BATHROOM) FOUND POETRY

This is the only real mark I'll ever make.

For once I have a pen
But I have nothing to say.

I just wrote on the wall
Take THAT Mom + Dad!

These are words above a toilet
In a high school
And therefore irrelevant.

I solemnly swear
I will not write on walls.

This is what we do because we can't VOTE.

I was going to write something profound
But I realized I have nothing profound to say.

Graffiti is lame.

The pen is mightier
Than nothing at all.

Ella is an irrelevant nobody
And not worth mentioning.

AFTER-SCHOOL SPECIAL

Samir gets a look sometimes
An another-time-zone look
He holds my hand
On his bare chest
His iron eyes
On the ceiling.

Do you ever think
About your brother?
I ask.
Do you read minds?
How did you know?

Marika's aide
Says I'm intuitive
I say.
Being with you
Makes me think
All kinds of things.
My mind becomes
Unshackled
And wild.

Do you ever write to him
Or email or call?
Samir shakes his head
Sitting up
Pulling on his T-shirt.

I've broken the spell
Somehow
But I don't care.

What's his name?
I ask.
Ash, Samir says
Ashraf.
He emails me sometimes.
I would call him
But my father
Forbids it.

He's buttoning his jeans.
Your father forbids
Many things, I say.
You do them anyway.
Samir does not
Smile.

ASH

The day he told us
My father cried
I had never seen him cry before

The day he left us
My father cursed him
In words he'd never used before

I love my brother
But I love my father too
And I never had to choose before

That day.

NEARLY FIFTEEN

Later I catch Kayli
Wrist deep
In my bedside table.
She laughs
A guilty laugh
And extracts a fistful
Of condoms.
You're too young
I say.
She sniffs
Nose in the air
A taste of snarky Kayli.
Don't sweetie, please
I try.
Is it Parker?
Is he pressuring you?
No pressure
No problem
None of your business.
She pockets the condoms
And promises
You tell, I tell.
And Samir will suffer
Worse than us.

Once, under
The crocheted blanket,
We swore

No man could
Come between us.
Once we vowed
It was me and her
Against Mom and Dad.
We were sisters in arms
United, blood-bound
Virgin warriors
Once.

PASTELS

I draw Kayli's pale, thin hand
Chipped pink nail polish and a
Fistful of stolen condoms.

In pretty pastels,
Like a greeting card you would
Give to your grandmother.

EUPHEMISTICALLY SPEAKING

I'm on Facebook when David's message pings
Do we need to talk, he writes
About the thing?

"The thing" where I kissed him on the steps
Two weeks have gone by already
Two weeks where we've run past each other
At school and barely stopped
To say hello.

Are we still friends, he writes
Or are we more?
I can't pretend like
Nothing happened.

Infuriatingly
My eyes fill up with tears
I'm supposed to be stronger than this
Colder, but instead I burn
Blushing with shame
Though there's no one around
To see it.

DISCRETION

I sniff back the tears
And write
"The thing?"
I like you.
What are you thinking?
Boyfriend/girlfriend?
Does it have to be public?
I'm not ashamed or anything.
I've just had enough of gossip.
A long time passes
With me choking
On my lies
Before David writes back
I'll see you at school.

411

It's not hard to find him
Ashraf combined with Samir's last name
And there's only one in New York.

And it's not hard to locate him
On Facebook, on Twitter, he even has a blog
With his graphic-design portfolio.

It's slightly hard to decide
The best way to contact him
Email, tweet, Facebook, comment on his blog?

It's hardest to know what to write
Hello, Ashraf, my name is Raphaelle
I'm secretly dating your brother Samir.

He misses you.

INSUFFICIENT

"Secretly dating"
Seems too small and innocent
For all that we are.

chapter five

DEFORESTATION

Apparently, every second
An area the size of
Two football fields
Is deforested.

That's horrible, of course
But when you think about it
Quite an achievement
Of man taming nature.

It's with this in mind
That I face the terror
Of having my bikini line pruned
And torn out by the roots
Like an unruly garden hedge.

I figure
If those Brazilians
Can cut down the Amazon
They can handle pretty much anything.

CLUELESS

My limping
Bowlegged return
Is met by Dad
And just-baked cookies.
Like he knows
Chocolate is the cure
For humiliation
And tender red skin.

What did you do today?
He asks in a kind of
Mindless parental mantra.
I wonder
If he really wants an answer
If asking satisfies
Some fatherly need
Or if he's waiting for me
To say something like

"I had most of the hair removed
Painfully
From my private parts.
What did YOU do?"

But I shove cookies in my mouth
And say, Shopping.

NUCLEAR TESTING

Then there is the matter
Of choosing a bikini.
Kayli has about a dozen

Each one
Tinier
Than
The
Last.

Why don't I just go nude?
That would cause a scene
Wouldn't be the first time
Kayli says, eyeing me
Assessing me
Narrow-eyed.

My flowered
Ample bottom
Overflows
My tidy boobs
Cower helplessly
Swathed in
Purple.

Can't I wear the WonderBra?
That gave me cleavage.
That's underwear, Ra
Is it a lingerie car wash?

We'd probably
Make more money
If it was.

Lingerie is hardly appropriate
Kayli pencils *A P P R O P R I A T E*
On her homework
And then

Sexy lingerie is not <u>appropriate</u> for teenage girls.

That's a vocabulary word
She says.

NOT QUITE IRISH TWINS

She:

Has golden light in her hair
Ocean-bright eyes
Dancer grace and athlete strength
Skin like butter
A pouting shape
Plentiful with promise.

I:

Have wiry mud waves
Storm-cloud eyes
Bones and butt and bloat
All in the wrong places
Skin like sifted flour
Dotted with spice.

She:

Can talk to anyone
And say nothing.

I:

Open my mouth
And obnoxious pours out.

She:

Was born silently in a warm bath.

I:

Was torn screaming into the world.

REFLECTION

My reflection glares
Flinging words
I try not to use.

Fat
Pale
Puffy

Disproportionate
Like I'm a badly executed
Painting.

My body
Swells
Distorts.

Once the me in the mirror
Was my golden temple
A swift and sturdy chariot.

Now she's becoming
My unwieldy burden
A suit of iron.

A twisted bitter sister
On whom bikinis
Shrink and choke.

She pushes me away
Holding me at arm's length
In her judgmental eye.

BROKEN MIRROR

And then
I want
To wrap
My naked
Body around
Samir's and
Let his
Ecstasy rebuild
The wholeness
Of me.

NEW EARTH

Our spring cleaning is a bit late
Because summer has fallen unexpectedly
Full-grown and armored
Into our unprepared laps.

Mom whistles as she rakes away
The last of the slush-mashed leaves
Now fragile, dry and cracked
By the relentless prairie sun.

Dad shreds papers and notes
Out-of-date progress reports
He won't need or prefers to forget
For the summer term.

Kayli piles unwanted clothes
And shoes on my stairs
Like her rejects, some unworn
Are good enough for me.

I sweat on my unmade bed
Choosing artwork from grade eleven
To add to my walls
Or discard.

The hand collection has grown
And is beginning to look
Peculiar, menacing even
Like an encroaching army.

The mandalas soothe me with their symmetry
But the portraits prickle my conscience
Sarah, I called Puffy and sketched
Fatter than she is.

Sarah and I might have been friends
In other circumstances
If I had achieved what I set out to do
Instead of what really happened.

How somehow I
Turned Genie against her
Tore them apart without even trying
Broke their BFF bond by being me.

My face gets hot.
The slant-ceilinged room is an oven
Even with the mudroom door open
Because heat rises and has nowhere to go.

SOIREE

They arrive in pairs
Or groups
Languid, drowsy-eyed
Arms slung over shoulders
Smelling mildly of skunk
And beer.
They call Dad "Drew" or "Boss"
And smoke in the driveway.

If they're graduates
Why are they still students?
Kayli asks.
She understands how it works
Just doesn't know why anyone
Would CHOOSE more school.

Two bearded boys slip out
Barefoot across the dewy yard
Fragrant tendrils of smoke
Curl above the back fence.
Want some?
Says one
When I join them
In the lane.

How old are you?
Says the other
As I puff

Inexpertly.
I would tell him
Or lie
I'm getting good at that
But I don't care
For the look on his face.

NIGHTTIME STROLL: PART ONE

Supposedly, it's safe
To walk at night
So I walk away
From the stoned
Graduate students.

Stay on the well-lit
Busy roads
Walk on the sidewalk
Squinting in the headlights
Trailing my hands
In the chain-link
Around the baseball field.

A shadow moves
Near first base
At first I think it's a child
But as it runs into the trees
I see its tail flick gray
Wait! I cry
As though a coyote
Would listen to me.

I try a tentative howl
Raising my face to the moon
My lungs sing and sear
And I run out of breath
But no one answers.

NIGHTTIME STROLL: PART TWO

David sniffs
Suspiciously
When I appear
Goose-bumped
And red-eyed
In his driveway.

You smell like weed
He says.
His brother, Michael
A taller, older lookalike
Dribbles a basketball
Like he doesn't care
About anything.

Dude, chill, he says
And grins at me
Where's the party?

My dad's students
Postgrads
Two of them
Were creeping me out
So I bailed.

It's not really true
They were harmless stoners
Historians in progress
How dangerous could they be?

But David softens
You walked here?
Do your parents know
Where you are?

No less than usual
I think.

CHIVALRY

And he walks me home
Because it's late
And he asks
For permission
Before giving me
A timid kiss
And he doesn't mention
I must taste of smoke
As we stand
Nose to nose.
And when the two stoners
Appear on the porch
And say, *Whoa*
You lucky bastard
David tells them
Laughing
To fuck off.
And I know
Later, maybe tomorrow
He'll ask me about it
And want to talk
About "us"
And I appreciate
That he knows
I'm too wasted
And tired
To discuss it now.

And I watch him
Amble away
Hands in pockets
Into the dark street
And I want so badly
To call him back
To call it all off
This selfish game
Right now.

BY THE WAY

Mouth fuzzy
Feeling like
A doppelganger
Is lying next to me
I (we) watch the moon
Traverse the skylight
And close my (our) eyes
Against the clawing
Accusing hands
Floating on a bed
Of paranoia.

So much
For not using
Drugs.

PLAYDATE

Samir brings his nephew
Jibreel, the angel
Who is nearly five months old.
You would never know
His shaky start to life.
I think of his tiny limbs
His bird's chest
Laced with tape and tubes.
Now he's round and rosy
Though still as bald as my
Newly waxed thighs.

Nina brings Aidan
Who emerged
More than fully cooked
Two weeks late, says Nina
They had to induce.
He's twice Jibreel's size
And crawling.

Marika and I sit on the patio
And watch the chaotic result.

Aidan squeezes Jibreel's fat foot
A little too hard.
Jibreel squeaks, kicks out
And Aidan cops it in the chin.
He cries until Jibreel farts

So loud I think they must hear it
On the Space Station.
Then they both laugh
Until they fall over.

NAP TIME

After Nina and Marika go
While Jibreel naps in his car seat
On the kitchen table
Samir slides his hand
Under my summer dress
And his fingers linger
On the surprising smoothness.

Can I look?
He asks
We slip behind the pantry door
Wow, he says
Admiring my new landscape
A neat and trim and tiny strip
You should take another picture
Like a before and after
Did you do this for me?

I could lie
And say yes
But do I really want him to think
I'm that kind of girl?

Then again
Is it better to be
The kind of girl
Who would
frolic practically naked
In front of strangers
For money?

PREDICTABLE

So I tell the truth
Experimentally
Like free-diving into open space.

Samir stares at me
His face unreadable
I watch him take two careful breaths.

Tell me you're kidding
He says, smoothing my dress down
And stepping into the kitchen.

And when I don't
He says something
I didn't realize I expected him to say.

What if I don't want you to?
He bites it back
But some things can never be unsaid.

He waits
As though he knows
The next words out of my mouth.

You don't own me
You don't control me
You can't tell me what to do with my body.

Jibreel coos

On the table

And saves us from ourselves, for now.

THERE IS NO ESCAPE

Yes, Ella
It has to be
A bikini
Otherwise it would be
A "Skanky Droopy
One-Piece Car Wash."

SECOND OPINION

David's only comment
About the car wash
Is that I should have fun
And remember
To wear sunscreen.

OASIS

Are you excited about summer?
Marika talks of nothing else
She has big plans for the two of you.

She knows I can't drive the van, right?

Marika loves taking the bus
And they all have ramps now
You'll be fine.

I'd like to do some art with her.

That would be great
You'd think she'd be sick of art
But she adores it.

I think she'll probably teach me things.

I wouldn't be surprised
She's studied all the techniques
Right now she's into Fauvism.

That suits me.
I'm quite wild myself.

CAFETERIALISM

I'm late for lunch
Because I fall into one of those
Moments where you just stare
Into your locker wondering
What is the meaning of it all?
And where is my Chapstick?

I sit with David
Although he's with his football friends
Who look at me like I have snakes for hair.
So, Ella, still doing photography?
One of them says
Dude, shut up, David says.

But I sweetly ask the friend
If he'd like to pose for a new piece
Called "Virgin Penises."
Don't qualify. But you could include David.
Oh my god. You're such a dick, David says
As his friends snicker into their smoothies.

Then I long to take David's hand
In front of everyone, even Samir
But instead I put both hands on my lap.
I hear you're doing the car wash, says the friend
Isn't a bikini a little overdressed for you?
David tenses but I shake my head.

It's not my style to have a boy fight for my honor
That's from songs and movies and trashy books
And I could probably eviscerate this douche nozzle
But I actually feel sorry for him
Because I'm pretty sure he's jealous
Of all that David has.

BROWN-PAPER PACKAGE

It arrives wrapped in plain brown paper
As though a vintage bikini is something
Kinky
Unseemly
Forbidden
I suppose for some people, maybe it is.

It's a little too big for me
In the boobs especially, but I fix it with
Pins
Darts
Tucks
And little hand stitches, like an Amish girl.

The blue polka-dotted high-waist bottoms
Cover everything
Belly
Navel
Ass
And every inch of waxed bit.

The intricately seamed and structured top piece
Turns my breasts into engineering wonders
Rockets
Missiles
Pleasure domes
I can't help but laugh at my pin-up self.

As usual, I look faintly ridiculous
Like a girl who has fallen out of time
And space
Into
Chaos
But at least, at last, I feel like me.

JUDGMENT

It's an odd vindication
To get the official report
On my grade-eleven year.

It's an odd evaluation:
Raphaelle overcame a lot
Of obstacles to get here.

It's an odd situation
Because the "obstacles" were set
By those who say, *We're proud of her.*

It's odd, their admiration
Those flaccid words they wrote
Instead of the truth that I'd prefer.

"Raphaelle is an abomination
A self-obsessed, destructive brat
A nihilist, a saboteur."

It's odd, the source of my salvation:
I passed all their tests, like that
Is any kind of accurate measure.

ESCAPE

We pour out doors
That open as though
For the first time
Freedom erupts
Shouts of triumph
Of primal joy
Rise into the blue sky.

I wonder, if we love summer so much
Why most of us will return.
The back-to-school magazines will arrive
And we will file obediently
Through those unlocked doors
Sucking down from the blue sky
Our triumph
Our joy
Our freedom
Letting the clouds of autumn fall
And close their dome around us.

For now I exhale and let
Stale repressive gym shoes
Linoleum wax
Trophy polish
Neglected books
Blue ink
Formaldehyde frogs
And whiteboard marker
Dissipate in the warm breeze.

I inhale one last breath
Of steel and concrete
Resolve and think
Just the car wash to survive
Now.

COLD AND DARK: PART ONE

We washed a hundred cars
And Genie glared
At my eye-popping attire.

And when the newspaper
Only wanted a picture of me
Looking like a manic vintage starlet

Genie glared some more.

We made good money
Secured away in Genie's car
With my backpack, clothes and phone.

The sun sank; it cooled off
And when the last water bucket was thrown
At me, it was all in fun.

Genie laughed first.

Then we all laughed as I dripped.
That makes me need to pee, I spluttered
And ran off past the Dumpsters

To the gas station bathroom
A seedy, creepy, damp and skeevy
Dingy cracked-white-tiled affair.

It smelled of mold and dead things.

I peed fast and wiped and washed
And rushed back to the parking lot to find
The girls, their cars, my clothes and phone

Their laughter
Those few hours of camaraderie
I worked so hard for

Gone.

chapter six

UNSEEN

COLD AND DARK: PART TWO

I could do it
Walk alone across town at night
In nothing but a vintage bikini
Floppy sun hat
And flowered flip-flops.

Or I could flounce into the Stop'n Go
Ignore the cashier's shocked stare
And demand to use the phone.

Or I could plead my case with a bus driver
And ask to borrow a sweater.

Or I could beg for quarters
And find a phone booth

And phone Samir or David
Or Ms. Sagal or Mom and Dad
And admit that here I am again.

Where girls I thought were becoming friends
Made off with my possessions
And left me to the concrete and steel.
I could just
Swallow
My
Shame.

But I can't move.

FROZEN

Like that girl
Locked under the stairs
In a condemned auditorium
In winter.

Frozen
Like an image
On a glitchy video
Me on the concrete, crying.

Frozen
Like that night
In the dark
I can't seem to leave behind.

Frozen
At fourteen nearly
Fifteen too scared to yell for help
Too drunk to think.

Frozen when they found me
Half dead, numb
With no words to explain
What happened.

Frozen
As their faces
When I finally
Went back to school.

Frozen as their lies
Tinkling down like icicles
We didn't realize
We thought you were right behind us.

Frozen
As a corpse on a mountainside
Maybe if they all want me dead
I should just die.

SPIRIT GUIDE

The gas station is out by the bypass on-ramp
So we would get the commuters heading home
Backing onto a fertilizer depot
That's out of business
With a narrow lane between them
Lined with rusty Dumpsters
I crouch between two of them watching
Truckers and strange shadowy men
Trudge past unbuckling
On the way to the bathroom.

I try to be quiet
Try to disappear into the dark
Bite down on my knuckles
To silence my chattering teeth
And time passes
The slice of dark sky above me changes
I watch Jupiter's transit
A satellite and a distant plane.

The cars on the highway hum
Until my ears ring so loudly
I can't hear my heart pound anymore
Maybe I fall asleep and dream
A tapping, scuffling noise
I turn my eyes up and see
I'm nose to nose with a coyote
Sniffing, she nods
Her primal understanding.

I would trade places with you
I tell her, I would trade bodies
She's wiry, lean and bright like
She drinks only moonlight, howling
Letting the white glow infuse her.
I would give my opposable thumb
And my dysfunctional frontal lobes
For her blurry fur,
Her bone-hungry freedom.

A car door slams
And she wisps away
Like smoke
Taking my dream with her.

NOT ALONE

Someone yells down the alley
And the hard steel rings
Like bells in my ears.

Footsteps crunch on gravel
Broken glass and oily trash
A low voice murmurs

A Dumpster lid creaks open
For a few seconds
And clangs shut

So loud it rattles something loose.
My mind clears
He sounds like he's praying.

Another Dumpster opens and
Closes like a gunshot.
He's praying.

I strain to hear over the trucks
And the blood rushing
I can't understand the words but

He's praying
Praying
In Arabic.

Samir.
My voice dies in my throat
I slam my fist on the metal.

He steps in front of the moon
And falls down, hand on his chest
Habibti, thank God.

You were looking for me in Dumpsters?
Why? I ask, and his eyes fill with tears.
Don't make me say it out loud.

MISSING GIRL

I've been looking for you for hours
Genie said you left her party.
You didn't answer your phone
No one is home at your place
I tried everywhere.

Twenty minutes ago Genie texted me
Admitting they left you here
That you were never at her house
That the last they saw of you
You were heading to the bathroom.

Put my hoodie on, you're shivering.
Alhamdulillah you're all right.
My heart is pounding
My heart, my love
I'll murder that sharmouta.

DAMAGE CONTROL

Please don't tell my parents
Don't tell anyone.
Not David
Not Kayli
No one.

I'd explain what this did to me
Last time
The long hours on a shrink's couch
The insomnia
But suddenly somehow our love seems
Fragile
Like we've crossed a bridge into a castle
Of cobwebs
And the slightest wind could blow us both
Away.

WHY?

Because I couldn't move
Because I was too embarrassed
Because I didn't know who to call.

You should have called ME, habibti
You can always call me, no matter what.

Because I thought you were mad at me
Because you didn't want me to do it
Because I don't like feeling that way.

What way? Like I care what happens to you?
Why would you want to show off like that?

Because I needed to join a group for the trip
Because once I'd joined I'd look chicken if I quit
Because I told myself I can do anything.

But how is that challenging for you?
Exposing your body like a stripper?

Because of what happened last year
Because I don't care if people see me
Because it's MY body.

But that was different; that was art
This was just trashy; you're better than that.

Because of this I didn't call you!
Because you think I'm trashy
Because maybe I belong in a Dumpster.

Raphaelle, my love, don't say that
You belong with me.

THE OFFICIAL STORY

How was the car wash?
Kayli asks
Though it's late
And hot in my room
She fell asleep in there
Waiting for me.

It was great, I lie
I went to Genie's after
And Samir picked me up
We went for falafel.

I hope that is the end of it
I can't do this again
Though Kayli is kind of innocent
Floating in her cloud
Of social success
It occurs to me
She might not know
The whole story
But I guess
That's how I like it.

Did Samir drop you off?
She asks
Dreamily
You're sleeping with him
Aren't you?
Is it good?

I don't answer
Thinking maybe
Nothing will ever
Be good again.

BEHIND MY EYELIDS

My eyes move
In dreams and I
Imagine my broken
Body, bikini askew
In the bottom of
A rusty Dumpster.

Time can't be undone
Mistakes can't be unmade
And the things Samir saw
Even if they weren't real
Can never be unseen.

FALLING WORDS

Like water rushing
Gushing
Over rocks
To froth and churn
Below.

Trashy.
Show-off.
Like a stripper.
And the word
He called Genie
Sharmouta
It means slut.

You can't trust
Girls like that
He said
Don't even speak to them
I'll get your clothes
And phone
Tomorrow.

Maybe everything
Will be better
Tomorrow

Maybe
Tomorrow
I won't be
A girl like that.

RED INK

I sketch
My hand
in red ink
Squeezing a sopping sponge
So the dripping water
Looks like blood.

HEAT

My clock says 12:03
When I wake
Baking
In the hot sun
Pouring in the skylight

Kayli is gone
The house is quiet
And my mind has flipped
Back to David.

EMPTY HOUSE

Kayli's room is cool
In both senses of the word
Cool as the permafrost
Two feet down
Cool as having the right handbag
The right haircut
The right shoes.

I lie on her wide pink bed
And imagine being the kind of girl
Who might sleep down here.
Sheathed in H&M pajamas
Powdered in pink
Circled in friends
Sweet but secretive.

Sweetness is something
I've never quite mastered
Never really wanted to.
But secrecy
Clings to me
As naturally as disaster
And humiliation.

Kayli found one of those
Ornate old phones
And hooked it up down here.
I wrap my fingers around

The curved handset
And think of phoning David
Wondering what I might say.

If I told him everything
About the girls in junior high
Who locked me in the dark
How I nearly died
About Genie's jealousy
And continued vengeance
Would he understand?

Or would he blame me too?

chapter seven

IMPRUDENT

KNEELING BUS

Buses kneel now, did you know?
Like supplicants
To Marika's regal glory
Bus drivers greet her like a queen
And flirt with us both.

She seems to know
Every person we meet
Young or old
From bald babies
To gray old ladies.

I

Will

Be

M-A-Y-O-R

One

Day

Marika says.
And no one disagrees.

TALKING

How was your first day with Marika?
Dad asks
Again with the uber-parenting
He smiles as I answer
Fine
Good
Fun.

I think this will be
A great summer for you, Rah Rah
He says
Oblivious.
A job, new friends
I hear the car wash was fun.
Mmm, I say
As he wanders off
Distracted by a ringing phone.

I could follow him
And tell him
How wrong he is.

But I can't
I've told Samir to forget it
He got my phone
And clothes back
And threatened Genie
To shut her up

And she has those other girls
Under her command.

No one else needs to know
No one needs my problems
Any more than I do.

I would talk
I could talk
I should talk
But I can talk
Myself
Out of talking
With anyone.

FULL DISCLOSURE

On the way back from 7-Eleven
With an after-dinner Slurpee
I run into Dad's student
The bearded stoner
Kieran is his name.
Silly, possibly imprudent
That I toke with him
In the park.
His smile slides smartly away
When I say "seventeen."

But he recovers.
How has your summer been so far?
Do you have a job?

Blearily
I tell him about Marika
And he says all kinds
Of patronizing things
About generosity
And what a good person
I must be to work with her.
This is news to me.
I thought I was doing it for money.

WHISPERS

Words waft up with heat waves
Trying to sleep with spinning things
Swimming in the water
In the ceiling.

Now I float feeling stupid
And clueless
But still the whispers drift, dancing
Up the stucco walls
To my window
Parker, no.

I sit up
Stand up
Kayli's voice on the front step
In the steamy air
The whole street watching her
Repeat *no*
I open my mouth to speak
But Kayli says *Just go*
Parker retreats
Conceding this battle
But maybe not
Admitting defeat.

Sweetie?
I call down
Are you okay?

But she disappears
Or doesn't hear
Or care
My thoughts tilt and melt
And sleep slips its
Slender arms
Around me.

DROPPED CALL

The home phone rings
And rings
And Mom picks it up
Hello?

No one there
She says with a shrug
But when it happens
Again

Does some boy
Have a secret crush
On you
Or your sister?

Crush? I say
Not that I know.
I don't tell her
I'm in on all the secrets.

FIRST BASE

Crack of ball on bat
David in his baseball hat
Me in cut-offs on a picnic mat.

He said he'd hit a homer for me
Like a teen TV movie parody
Those ones that end in tragedy.

But a sticky orange Popsicle
The heat rising like it's tropical
Makes the summer afternoon magical

For today no one gets caught by lies
No one gets hit by a ball and dies
And no one tells secrets or cries.

EVASION

I like pizza
And boys
Together especially.

Though sometimes I prefer boys
With their mouths full of pizza
Than asking awkward questions.

Like *are we a couple?*
And *why are you so afraid*
Of being normal?

And if I could list
All the reasons I'm afraid
It might take my whole life.

Instead
I almost tell David
That I love him.

I love him for
What he doesn't know
About me.

FILE MANAGEMENT

                        things
            the   I
            though   almost
      as   say
      feel   are
      to   piling
   starting   too
   I'm   high

THE BOOK OF MORMON CAMPING

It sounds like a nightmare to me
But "all denominations are welcome"
And Kayli doesn't want to face
Two weeks without Parker
Her deceptively proper and polite
Mormon boyfriend
Who I happen to know
Has reached second base at least.

Two weeks of tall trees
A green lake
Campfires
Lumpy bunks
And sneaking into shadows
For fumbling frolics
In fragrant piles
Of pine needles.

Please oh please oh please
Kayli says
I promise I'll pass
All my classes.
I pinky promise.
Pinky promises bear no weight
With Mom
But Dad is moved

By Kayli's earnest entreating.
Mormons, Mom says later
They'll suck her in
To their bizarro world.
Then she changes,
Puts on her church dress
And drags Dad and Kayli
To the house of our God.

LUNGS

We all pretend not to listen
To Kayli breathe
Mom especially
Stops
Talking

In the middle of sentences
And waits while Kayli
Ties her shoes
Or pours juice
Listening

Trying to hear
The telltale hiss
Like a punctured tire
A gas leak
Something toxic

It's usually mild
"Mild," they say at the ER
Except when it's not
Except when it's
Catastrophic

I pretend not to listen
To the panic in Mom's voice
Next year, she says
Or the year after
Like things will be different

Mom trusts God
To help and support her
Help Kayli breathe
Whatever it takes
But she doesn't trust God

Enough.

CAPRICIOUS: PART ONE

Like all good Catholics
Mom is obsessed with death
She reads the obituaries
From back home
And visits graveyards
With bunches of daisies
Picked in the lane.

We got Charlotte a headstone
She tells me
About a homeless woman
Who died last New Year's
Frozen like leftovers
Resplendently dead
On a park bench
With a book I gave her
Tucked in her pale hand.

Charlotte rests
Under a scrawny tree
And I nearly break my ankle
In a gopher hole
On the way to her grave.
I see a golf ball
Two condoms
And a child's mitten
Squashed in the mud.

Mom lays the daisies
On the stone
And murmurs a prayer
While I hear the clang
Of a Dumpster closing
The cars on the highway
And wonder what
Charlotte ever did
To God.

AN ANSWER

Dear Raphaelle,

Thank you for writing. Samir and I haven't spoken in years.
I email him on his birthday, and other days.
I miss him too. I miss my whole family.

I appreciate what you are trying to do, but I think it's hopeless.
Some chasms can never be crossed.

I've thought about calling Sam.
I imagine he has his own cell phone now.
It's not my place to ask you for his number,
but I'd love to speak to him
Even for a few minutes. You could give him my number too.

Please don't think badly of him for this.
Family comes first to him.
To me too, but I can't change who I am.

All the best,
Ashraf

NOT YOUR BUSINESS

Samir looks left then right
Then plants a kiss on me
Behind Starbucks.

Samir looks intent
When he reads the email
On my phone

Samir looks at his feet
When he tells me
I don't understand.

Samir looks at his watch
And I remind him
I lost a brother once.

He lived and died
In the time it takes
To tell his story.

We look at each other
Across that chasm
Ashraf described.

DUSK

The sun skims along the horizon

Rolling slowly like a ball neglected
Slipping into the earth reluctant

Darkness trickles over houses

Leeching colors from lawns sighing
And cooling the air relieved

My feet turn me away from home

And past sprinklers going *tsk tsk tsk tsk*
As though they know my destination

Is David's house.

WITNESS

It's hard to watch someone you love
Watch someone they love
Fall apart.

Like all those times with Mom
Catching her
Weighing herself
For the fourth time that day
Watching her eat
Or not eat
And the way Dad looked at me
When she'd abandon dinner
It was hard to watch him
Watch her leave.

David beseeches his raving brother
To come inside
Hey, Ella, whazzup?
Michael slurs at me
Blinking and twitching
Let's go party.
And he yanks my hand so hard
I stumble onto the grass.

Whoa, sorry, Michael says
And helps me up
That was uncool.
David doesn't move
He doesn't speak

It's hard to watch him
Watch this colossal wreck
This giant idol
Tumble over in the dust
Like Ozymandias.

Michael pulls his shirt off
Hey, Ella, let's moonbathe
He says and lies down
On the driveway.
His rib bones outline a history
Of self-neglect.

Come inside, David whispers
I'm not sure to whom.

CONFIDE IN ME

It started again
At college
He dropped out
And came home
And seemed to get better.
But lately he's relapsed
I guess.
Relapsed.
I really never thought
I'd have to use that word.
And he's nineteen now
So we can't force him into rehab
Like last time.
Rehab.
Another word I never thought I'd need.
And now you're looking at me
Like "why didn't you tell me this
Before now?"
The thing is it's not every day
Sometimes he's like my brother
We shoot hoops and watch hockey
But sometimes he loses it
And runs off
Somewhere
Then he usually texts me
And I go pick him up
And he's like this.

ADVICE I COULD GIVE MY SISTER

They tell you boys will take what they want
From your body and leave you with nothing
But tears and unwanted babies, but really boys
Take much more (if you let them) from your heart.

They tell you to be strong and independent and
Decide where and when you want to give that
Part, but really you need to be strong enough for
Two because every feeling he'll need to share.

And he will be as helpless as that unwanted baby
In the face of sadness or regret or worry or anger
He won't know what to do unless you tell him and
Then you have to be prepared for him to blame you

When it all goes to hell.

COFFEE

Samir and I
Have coffee
Before his shift.
Him struggling
To not touch me
Me struggling
To wake up.

I rub my eyes
And focusing
See Genie.
The door swings closed
Behind her
And Samir
Seeing my expression
Spins.

Do you want me
To kick her out?
He asks.

She gets in line
Glancing my way.
The line moves slowly
I'll kick her the fuck out
Samir whispers
I don't care
What it looks like.

The line moves
She glances.
I still haven't
Remembered how
To speak.
Tell me what to do
Samir says.
Nothing, I manage
It's fine.

It's not fine.
She glances my way
Halfway down the line
Then, coffee-less, turns
And leaves.

TEXT FROM DAVID

Can't do lunch.
Looking for Michael.
Again.
Sorry.

HONESTY

I ask Marika
Is it wrong
To bail on someone you care about
Because you don't want
To deal with their problems?

Yes.

I-M-A-G-I-N-E

If

Mom

Had

B-A-I-L-E-D

On

Me.

I ask Marika
Is it wrong
To tell people
Everything's fine
When it's not?

S-T-U-P-I-D

Not

Wrong.

I ask
Is it wrong to have sex with one boy
When you are falling in love
With another?

She takes her time answering.

Wrong

And And And And

A-N-D

Stupid.

WISDOM

You

Are

S-E-L-F - D-E-S-T-R-U-C-T-I-V-E

For

All

The

Wrong

R-E-A-S-O-N-S

You

Think

The

World

Is

Out

To

H-U-R-T

You

So

You

Want

To

Get

There

F-I-R-S-T.

chapter eight

UNFINISHED

LAST MINUTE (S)MOTHERING

Do you have batteries
For the nebulizer?
Do you have the vials?
Your spare inhalers?
How far away is the clinic?
What's the phone number?
Drew, did you write it down?
What's the camp nurse's name?
Do you have sanitary pads?
Bug spray?
Sunscreen?
Band-Aids?
Socks?
Sunglasses?
A hat?
Do you have a hat?
Do you have our cell numbers?
Do you really have to go?

TURN SIGNAL

She watches the car
Until the traffic lights change
And Dad turns left
Toward the highway
Out of town
Out of her reach.

It's only two weeks, I say

She watches the corner
As the traffic lights change
Do you want to make lemonade?
I ask, her back turned to me
I wonder if it was me in the car
How long would she watch?

It's only two weeks, I think

Maybe Mom doesn't quite
Understand what I've lost too
My best and only girlfriend
The one who might listen
And snort with sympathetic outrage
If I ever gathered the courage

To tell her.

BRUSH AND INK

If Marika notices my silence
She makes no comment
Maybe in listening to my nothing
She catches the truth of me.

She makes no comment
When I press my brush to paper
And leave a shapeless blob
A spreading black stain.

Maybe in listening to my nothing
Something shouts of joy or darkness
Marika sees more than brush and ink
In my uncertain unmoving hand.

She catches the truth of me
The volumes of lore stacked on shelves
She'll find an unmanageable archive
If Marika notices my silence.

MORE SILENCE

When I get home
Mom is tutoring Nina
Aidan asleep in his stroller
Dad is in his study
Door closed.

I pour a glass of milk
In the empty kitchen
Adding things to the pile
Of stuff I really need to say.

Mom, I'm sleeping with Samir
Dad, David's brother is a drug addict
Mom, Samir's gay brother misses him
Dad, I think Kayli's boyfriend is a jerk.

I feel like I'm going crazy again.
Mom? Dad?

THE GIFT

Text from Samir:

OK, I'll call Ash 2morrow. 4 u.

Text from Ella:

Yay! What made u change your mind?

Text from Samir:

Jibreel asleep in my lap.
Love u.

DRIVING TEST: PART TWO

Last time
I ran a stop sign
Which is an automatic

Fail

And Dad said
Everybody fails first time out
And Mom said
You've got all summer to practice
And Kayli said
Did you hit anyone?
And I said

No

And I didn't say
That I ran the stop sign
Because I didn't see it
Because my eyes were full of

Tears

This time David brings me
Michael's car is smaller
Easier to drive
And he waits while I go inside
And fill out a form

And take a number
Only before my number comes up
I walk back out to his car
And buckle up staring at

Nothing

Okay, he says, *okay*
And we drive

Away

HE TRIES

I know something is bothering you
I wish you would tell me what
I'm not one of those intuitive guys
I'm not sure there is such a thing

I know something is bothering you
And I'm worried it's about us
But it's okay if you're not sure
We could take things slowly

I know something is bothering you
Is it your job or your parents?
I understand how painful both can be
You know I really like you, right?

I mean as more than a friend
But we're still friends too
If that's what you need because
I know something is bothering you.

SOMETHING

Itchy
Dirty
Like my skin
Is choking me
Like my limbs don't fit
Like I'm not a person
Like I'm watching the world
Through someone else's eyes.
Tired
Sad
Like I'll never do another
Interesting thing.
Like all I am is
Some girl to leave behind
Like trash
Like one of those
Missing kids
On milk cartons.
Lost
Alone
And unable to move
Or speak.

DAWN

So early that I haven't slept
When the sky brightens
My curtains and it
Must be a million degrees
I swear I'm swimming
In sweat.

So early that in the half
Awake I forget the
Reasons I sometimes
Dread the day, the
Effort to repress
My regrets.

So early that the birds
Are quiet still
They haven't yet
Awoken to the cats
Who stalk their
Drowsiness.

So early that
Yesterday seems too
Close to unfinished
Like time is overtaking
Me, a runner in a race
I didn't mean to enter.

MONEY

Another day with Marika
Unable to resist her joy
I'm slightly exhausted
Face sore from laughing
Down by the lake.
We watched ducks and boys
And agreed we prefer ducks
Because they're smarter
And have

C-L-E-A-N-E-R

Feet.

Ms. Sagal pays me with a check
I bank it, withdrawing twenty dollars
And blow it all at the thrift store
Under the church on Cornwall
Everything black, a little
Vintage funeral dress
A tiny men's tuxedo jacket
A long witchy skirt.
A T-shirt of an '80s band
No one remembers.

At Starbucks
Samir buys me an iced tea
And we sit on the patio

While he tells me that his brother
Told him that he's marrying
Another man in New York.
I ask him how he feels
And he says
Dead inside.

REALITY CHECK

What He Could Have Said:

"I'm so happy for him
I hope I can go to the wedding
It was great to talk to him
He seems to be in a good place
The guy, Ben, sounds nice
I can't wait to tell my sister
She'll be thrilled."

What He Did Say:

I sort of wish I'd never called him
I mean, what's the point?
How am I supposed to react to that?
I know he didn't choose to be gay
But he could be discreet about it
Now I have this hanging over me
And I can't tell anyone but you.

JUST HOW SHALLOW AM I?

The thing to do
When I get home
Would be to call David
Isn't that the point?
To Frankenstein
Two boys together
Making a perfect boyfriend?

Wasn't the idea
To let them fill the gaps
In each other?
David's tolerance tempers
Samir's passion
David's passivity stirred
By Samir's urgency.

But the whole of them
Is starting to feel less
Than the sum of them
And the whole of me
Is starting to feel
Much too
Small.

DATE NIGHT

Kieran appears at the door
Dad's grad student
I say
Mom and Dad are out
And he gives me
A bundle of papers
Which I should just
Shove into Dad's office
And say good night
But instead I ask him in.

Want to get high?
He says
We pad across the
Cool grass to the alley
Startling a raccoon
Kieran's match
Lights up the tiny
Footprints in the dust.

Smoke settles
Around me like a halo
This time it
Feels something like
The unscrewing of a vise
Grip deep inside
My head.

Seventeen, Kieran says
Fingering a strand of my hair
I'm twenty-three
So I feel like
Quite the pervert
Right about now.

Yeah, I say.
Come see my room.

ART SHOW

You did all these?
Some of them are pretty good
I like the mandalas
And this Jesus one.
It's Jesus, right?

It sort of creeps me out
Was that the idea?
Like he's watching
And I don't know
Judging.

And the hands are weird
Who is the one with the key?
Your art teacher, huh.
What does the key mean?
Some kind of metaphor?

Wow, that shit was strong
I'm flying here and
You look like you're falling
Asleep or waiting
For me to kiss you.

No offense
You know you're sort of cute
In a vintage jailbait kind of way
But your dad would kill me
AND fail me.

I think you're playing grown-up
And I don't feel that grown-up myself.
So maybe I'm not the right guy for your game
Besides, this scared-rabbit thing you're doing
Right now is really not that sexy.

MUNCHIES

He disappears down the stairs
Don't tell your dad, okay?
He calls back.
I mean, I didn't do anything
Except get you high
But still.

Please, I say
What do you think I am?
He doesn't answer
Just slams the door
But my own buzzing skull
Has plenty to say.

I suppose I could
Go downstairs
And eat everything
And slink back up
To vomit technicolor
Humiliation.

Instead, I write a list.
NO more drugs
NO more self-pity
NO staying up all night
WHAT am I doing?
STOP asking for trouble

STOP being so stupid
STOP being so selfish
STOP looking in the mirror
STOP obsessing
About everything
SCREW those bitches.

NEW YORK, I write
EARN MONEY
GET THROUGH GRADE TWELVE
COLLEGE somewhere not here
And *FIX THIS MESS*
Though I have no idea

How.

CRAYON

Kieran's fingers
I scratch them in green
Smudgy crayon
With black charcoal
Rubbed in
On a crumpled sheet
Torn from an old
History handout
Like a zombie hand
Pulling me by the hair
To the land of the dead.

ALWAYS DARKEST

When Samir nudges me awake
The clock reads 2:04 AM
The mudroom door was unlocked
He says
Is it okay if I stay?

He's sweaty and hot
He must have jogged
The whole way
After all that effort
How can I turn him away?

Anyway, his arms
His lips, his tongue
And the rest of him
Are exactly the fix
I need.

WHISPERS

Samir, I whisper
He stirs and turns to face me
Moonlight in his eyes.

Do you remember
Last year when things fell apart
How the whole world knew?

I think that might be
Much better than this secret
Storm inside of me.

Habibti, what storm?
You mean about the car wash?
My love, please don't cry.

What is it about
Me that inspires such contempt?
Did they want me dead?

That was just so cruel
Way beyond the normal cruel
And far into malice.

I can't stop thinking
Of ways to balance it out
Even things again.

You mean like revenge?
Both your religion and mine
Advise against it.

Not revenge so much as
Correction, erasure to
Somehow rewind time.

Time can't be undone
And mistakes can't be unmade
But God will judge them.

That would comfort me
As Samir sleeps if only
I believed in God.

chapter nine

UNFEELING

CAREER ASPIRATIONS

So	What	is grown up?
	Do	you get some kind of card?
	You	know, like a bus pass?
What if I don't	Want	it?
	To	grow up at all
Much less	Be	something
	When	I do?
How do	You	know when it's time to
	Grow	up?
And is	Up	the only direction?

PLANNING

Mom leaves my enrolment form on the counter
With certain things circled and labeled
AP classes: English, History, Art
Easy A is the annotation on these
Chemistry, Physics, Biology
Medical school, she notes.
Medical school!
Calculus—*challenging*
No kidding.
French—*oui?*
Non, I inscribe.

I stare out the back window
At the yard baking in the sun
And imagine my grade-twelve year
As a kind of dystopian death match
Where students write florid essays
In the blood of their fallen classmates
Where *I*s are dotted with bullet holes
And *T*s are crossed with tears.

I would think of my future
My aspirations
I DO have them
Somewhere under all of this
I would make the connection between school
And future the way I'm supposed to

But when I think of school all I see
Is smirking spiteful girls
And two clueless boys
Who can never be enough
To protect me.

And when I think of the future
Beyond school it looks
Dangerous, like a destination
I haven't packed for
Like I've arrived in Siberia with
A suitcase full of sarongs and flip-flops
Sunscreen and beach towel
Bikinis and a pink chiffon dress
Like I might just walk out
Into the arctic snow and
Lie down and freeze.

THINGS I'LL CHANGE ABOUT MYSELF IF I GET THE TIME

I'll rejoin the human race
I'll try some makeup on my face
A little liner around the eyes
I'll drop a dress size
Give up chocolate, chips and pop
Maybe give my shitty hair a chop
Layers or bangs, a stylish bob
Stop being such a thrift-store slob
Buy something from The Gap
Throw out all that vintage crap
Make some friends, ones with cars
Go to parties, sneak into bars
Probably take up heavy drinking
Try to stop the neurotic thinking
Become the kind of person I can love
That Mom and Dad can be proud of.

EXCUSES

David is never late
Except when he is
Greeting me with profuse
Apologies and vague
Explanations as though I
Don't know that something
Happened with his brother
This time in the middle of
The day, which can't be good.

For some reason screwing up
At night is more socially acceptable
It's not logical because darkness
Is dangerous: you're more likely
To walk into traffic or fall into
The lake or freeze on a park bench
Or be jumped, mugged, raped, murdered
Tossed into a Dumpster with
Other broken discarded stuff.

He nudges my knee and takes
My hand but under the table like I
Asked him to once and gives it a
Little squeeze before letting go
Are you okay? You're spacing out
I'm worried about Michael, I say
And it's not a lie so much as
Only part of the whole truth.

FALLEN ANGEL

Michael lies on the lawn
Behind the house
Arms and legs out
Like a starfish drying
Dying on a rock.

He smells pretty bad
David says
I send him inside
For a glass of water
And help Michael sit up.

Let's take this off, I say
He lets me remove
The puke-ripe T-shirt
And slumps there
As I toss it away

His spine curled
Each vertebra like a knife
That might cut him open
From the inside.
Jesus, David says.

Michael drinks the water
Where's your mom?
I ask David. He shakes
His head. *She's done
With me*, Michael says.

Dad won't even let him
In his apartment anymore
I help David bring him inside
And lay him out on his bed
Surrounded by towels.

You should go, David says
Mom will come home
I suppose eventually
She'll be embarrassed
If she finds out you know.

But I sit and hold his hand
And let the hours pass
Watching his brother
Roil and heave like lava downhill
Burning everything in its path.

BENEDICTION

Ella, you're a sweet girl
And brave too. I think some chicks
Would run a mile, even from a catch like David
When they saw he's related to me.

Brother, you're a lucky guy
You found her without even trying
And after all you did to screw it up
She's still holding your hand over me.

Ella, you're a sweet girl
For knowing all I need is a glass of water
And towels, somewhere to sleep
And someone to watch me breathe.

Brother, you're a lucky guy
Hold on to her tightly and don't let go
There are streaks of light and dark in her
But both are good, and necessary.

Did you know that life depends on change?
On day and night, on seasons?
On the rotating Earth? On the orbiting planets?
That stillness equals death?

Do you know how orbits work?
Gravity and velocity seem like enemies

But really they're partners together
Making something that seems like magic

I'm raving again, aren't I?
I do that sometimes when I'm searching
For answers, for reasons why I'm falling
That's all an orbit is: it's falling.

Did you know in a vacuum
A parachute would be useless?

Ella, you're a sweet girl.

Brother, I promise this is the last time.

ACRYLIC

Michael's fingers
All bones and skin
Scraped knuckles
Raw, chewed fingertips like
Maybe a rat nibbled at him
While he was passed out somewhere.
There's dirt under his nails
As though he's been buried alive.

I paint it on a tiny canvas
In garish Fauvist colors
Trying to inject life
Into his corpse-like flesh.

LACE

Marika wants a push-up bra
But her mom won't buy her one

I'm

Not

Too

Young

She says
I don't disagree
Only the store that sells
Bras for small-titted teens
Is also where
Genie works.

Hi, Marika!
She says
When we find her
Among the fronds of pink
And lace.
Hi, Ella, she adds
Quickly
Her eyes averted
As though even to greet me
Is a lie.

She wants to buy a bra, I say
And Marika glares at me
Because she prefers
To speak for herself.

Genie, the queen of glares
Doesn't notice
She only gasps
How fun!
Can I help you choose?
And they roll off.

When it's time to fit
Marika waves me away
And lets the expert dress her.
And the two of them
In the accessible fitting room
Giggle and squeal.

While I panic.

PANIC

And I mean panic
Cold sweat
Hot flush
I clutch a rack
Of thongs
And try to blink
Away the black
Gathering at the edge
Of my vision.

Would you like to sit?
Genie's colleague says
And offers a baroque chair
I slump there like a bug
Dying on a rosebud.

When Marika surfaces
I help her get out her money
And the cashier rings up her two bras
One white, one black.

Genie kisses Marika's cheek
And doesn't say another word
To me before she
Disappears.

INTUITION

A few stores later Marika stops

What

Is

Wrong?

Nothing, I say and pretend to look
At the kind of shoes I'd never wear.

Lie

To

S-O-M-E-O-N-E

Else

Not

Me

It's private, I finally come up with
Marika manages a doubtful look
And types

I

Am

A

Good

L-I-S-T-E-N-E-R

But I have nothing to say.

A VACUUM

I can't complain to her of all people

A girl who can barely move or speak
Marika might listen but she would never understand

No word exists to encompass what is wrong. I know I'm
Obnoxious. I know I upset people. I get
That. I really do though sometimes I'm not sure
How it happens. It's not that I don't care for people. Obviously
I do. I try to anyway. I try to see the sadness in them and
Not judge their unwillingness or inability to see the
Goodness, the worth, in the vacuum of space in me.

But hurts like mine are easily hidden behind laughter or
Under ugly ill-fitting clothes or artwork
Too obscene to display in public.

Trying to tell Marika what lurks in the dark
Recesses of me is more than confession, it's
Asking her for absolution for my
Stupidity. As though her forgiveness might undo the
Heresy of me in a vintage bikini.

EMPTY HOUSE

I come home to a note.
Obviously, Mom has forgotten
About cell phones.
Again.

Don't worry. Your sister is fine.
She had a bad asthma attack.
They took her to hospital.
Dad and I are driving up there.
Everything is fine. Don't worry.
There are pizzas in the freezer.
We'll call later.
Don't worry.

Don't worry
Like worry can be turned on
And off like a TV
And after pacing for two hours
And eating every chocolate chip in the house
I call Samir, who comes over
To worry with me
Until our bodies overtake our minds.

A SONNET TO ENDINGS

The darkest part of night is when I plan
Outlining words, excuses and remorse
I'll try to spare his feelings if I can
I don't know how without more lies. Of course
There will be tears; most likely they'll be mine
But I deserve the punishment. I guess
I made this bed myself and now it's time
To lie in it and hope to convalesce.
My love was complicated but sincere
As much as it is possible to hold
Two boys. But I should face my biggest fear
Alone. It's not so much about the cold
Unfeeling world as MY unfeeling heart
That elevates capriciousness to art.

IT'S LONELY IN THE DARK

For no specific reason
My heart starts to race
In the dark.

Samir sleeps beside me
A little smile on his face.
Somewhere in New York
His brother sleeps
Next to his beloved
And Kayli sleeps, I hope
With the nebulizer mask
And Mom sleeps in a chair
And Dad, knowing him
Is asleep in the car.
And David sleeps
Maybe.

The whole world slumbers
Unaware of all the things
I'd never say.

ANOTHER SECRET

On
      My
            Birthday
Kayli pushed me
Down the basement stairs
We called her Michaela then
Back when we were both cherubs

Kayli
      Shoved
            Me
Because I turned ten
And got my ears pierced
Two tiny green peridot studs
For making it into double digits.

She
      Cried
            When
I couldn't stand
Get up, get up, get up
And I swore I would never tell
And I didn't tell, I only said I fell

I
      Never
            Told
What part of it hurt the most

That she pushed me and called me fat
How her envy had poisoned her that instant
And turned her feathered bright white wings to ash.

My

      Little

           Sister

I was proud of those earrings
Turning them, wincing and diligent until
The day Mom said my ears were nicely healed
I pulled them out and I threw them down the drain.

WATERCOLORS

Mom's hand
Flat, facing me
As if to say
STOP TALKING

And Dad's hand
Flat, facing me
As if to say
Just let me finish this

I dig through my craft box
And decorate each hand
With a tiny peridot sequin
In the center of the palm.

I recognize them
Too late
As those hands
That ward off evil.

Samir has one
Hanging in his kitchen
He told me what they're called
But I forget.

EPIPHANY

What if this is true:
Everything bad that happens
Is really my fault?

SHORTNESS OF BREATH

At last my phone rings.
Yo, it's me, Kayli says
Way to let the parentals freak out.
Why didn't you stop them?
Now I'm stuck here
In this backwoods chop shop
While someone decides
If I have pneumonia.
Pneumonia?
I don't have freaking pneumonia
      It's a cold, Mom, a chesty cold.
This is ridiculous.
They don't want me to
Make the drive home.
They talked about using "Child Flight"
Child Flight?! How embarrassing.
How are you anyway?
Beside me, Samir stirs
And opens his eyes.
I'm fine, I say
My hand over his mouth.
When are you coming back?
Who knows?
      Mom? When can we go?
Tomorrow or the next day.
They're not letting me go back to camp.
I don't really care though
Because Parker has turned into

A fart-sucking douche face.
        Mom! It's a private conversation
        With my sister.
What happened? What did he do?
I'll tell you later
Mom's still listening
        Well? You are!
I should go. Love you, Rah Rah
Don't forget to eat
And you know
Use condoms.
        Mom! Chill. I'm joking.
Later, loser. No. Wait.
I'M the loser.

PLAYING GROWN-UP

We spend the day together
Quiet as a married couple
Who have amicably
Run out of things to say.

The words I planned dissolve
Under his warm hand
On the curve of my back
In the sunshine
The day rises and falls
Like a last breath.

Toes touching
I read a fat newspaper
While Samir kills zombies
And when it seems the time
Will never be right
David calls.

THE SEARCH

Samir drives
His earlier cordial silence
Replaced with sulk
To be fair it is
After midnight
And three hours
Into a tour
Of the shitty parts of town
Searching for someone
Samir doesn't know
Who is the brother of
Someone he does who
Is kind of my other
Boyfriend.

He looks just like David
Only skinny
I tell Samir
All I get is a grunt
As he gazes through the windshield
At a group of goth girls
Wreathed with smoke
Thank you for helping me
I try and he gives
My knee a pat.

I'm at the park
A text from David reads
Be careful, I text back
And direct Samir to a corner
Where everyone knows
The tweakers hang out
Meth? Samir asks
Why would anyone do it?
He's sad, I guess
What does he have
To be sad about?

ADDICTION

What do any of us
Have to be sad about?
Except that feeling of
Waking up from a dream
And realizing everything
We thought was real
Is fantasy?

These skin and bones
These wraiths stripped
Off all that artifice
Freed the coyote in them
Became moonlight
And hunger in the
Moment dwelling
Visionaries who see
Only with their eyes.

The world is not
A nice place I tell Samir
As though he doesn't know.

THE END OF TIME

Is that him? Samir asks
Of a tall shadow
Near the park entrance.

I can see it's David
But a moment of Michael
Washes over him like
A projected ghostly
Skeleton.

Anything?
David asks as we join him
And accepts our answer
With stoic resignation.

He's probably just sleeping it off somewhere
Samir says
To fill the silence
To reassure.

But David's phone rings
And everything good
Evaporates.

PERSEVERATION

Is he dead?
David says
I slide my arms
Around his waist
And hold tight.

Is he dead?
Samir hangs his head
His own brother
A swirling cloud
Around him.

Is he dead?
My breath reaches
Across the plains
To Kayli's damp lungs
Filling them.

Is he dead?
No, I'm not coming
To the hospital
Until you tell me
If he's dead.

IS HE DEAD?
And Michael's gravity
Pulls us both down
Knees to concrete far
Too heavy for me.

TICKING AWAY

Time
Takes no prisoners
Trailing behind
Samir's car like a
Slipstream mist.

Not enough time
To gather the bits
Of David sufficiently
To get him to
What's left of his
Family.

We need more time
To capture the tears
Even Samir is crying
Wiping his eyes
As he drives blind in
The dark damp streets
Slower than time.

I've run out of time
David kisses me
In the backseat
Smothering sobs
On my lips. Stop
I whisper, stop this
You don't know
What you're doing.

This time
Samir pulls the hand brake
And yanks David's collar
Dude, calm down
She said stop.
Their eyes meet
And the look they share
Tells me my time
Has come.

HOW NOT TO SAY GOODBYE

The rest of the drive drowns
In one of those silences that suffocate.
David curls up against the door
Trembling, his face tucked into
The crook of his elbow.

Samir stares at the road
Lips parted in a protest
An accusation or
Condemnation
That has yet to find the words.
His eyes are as dry
As my mouth.

The white light of the ER entrance
Silhouettes the tall shape
Of an uncle or father
That gathers David as
I step out of the car.
You must be Ella, the shape says.
Not a father then
Since David's father knows me
All too well.

Is Michael dead?
I say, because David was never able to
Speak the words.
The shadow speaks for him.
Yes, I'm afraid he is.

STATE OF NOT BEING

Yes	I'm still thinking of myself
I'm	turning away
Afraid	to watch whoever this is as
He	leads David into a world where Michael
Is	no more

PARKED

Just tell me this one thing
Have you been with him all along?
Since that day on your stairs?
Since you told me he was just a friend?

Come inside, come upstairs with me, please

Do you think that's how it works?
Is that what you think of me?
That I'll forget what just happened
If you take off all your clothes?

Please just let me try to explain, please

What possible explanation could there be?
We have been together like man and wife.
You told me, repeatedly, that you love me.
Is this what you call love?

I do love you. I promise you, that's true

It's a sin, what we have done together,
I should marry you and make it right
But how can I trust you ever again?
You're completely crazy! Why would you do this?

I don't know.

I don't know.

I don't know.

EXIT

He reaches past me
And pushes open my door
Everything he wanted to say
He has said.

I plead from the sidewalk
Please, Samir
You're in no state
To drive.

Close the door
He says
And when I do
He drives
Slowly
Away.

LIES

Every time I told him
David is just a friend
Every time I told David
Samir and I are over

Every lie I told
To support this experiment
To entertain myself
Throbs in my brain

Every person I care about
Floats before my eyes
Like a video game
Played by God and me.

He smites them. I hurt them.
The points add up.
Smite. Michael dies.
Hurt. Samir cries.

Smite. Kayli's lungs.
Hurt. David's trust.
Smite. Marika's brain.
Hurt. Puffy's portrait.

Smite. Charlotte dies.
Hurt. Mom believes my lies.
Smite. We lose baby Gabriel.
Hurt. I try to seduce one of Dad's students.

And all the people I just *want* to hurt.
I'm jealous of Kayli
I hate Genie for what she did
I hate all those car-wash girls

And school, and teachers and principals
And those bitches in junior high
And Samir's family and God
And the one I hate the most of all:

Me.

chapter ten

INDISCREET

REASON

Sometimes
When people speak
To me of God my eyes
Fill with tears of loss.
As though they are talking
About some kid who died young
From drugs or guns.
As though someone I loved
Who I once thought loved me too
Was an illusion.
How can I mourn him
The imaginary friend
Who was never real?

MOM'S BATHROOM

Last Christmas
I found her in here
Unconscious
In a puddle of blood
And vomit
That's not something
You easily forget.

The white tiles shine
No evidence is left
I scrubbed this floor
Until my fingers ached
And stung from bleach
But the image remains
Like permanent marker
Scrawled graffiti
In my brain.

Tucked behind her closet
It has no windows
And if I close the door
I can imagine I'm
Flying through space
Alone past the heliopause
Outside the influence
Of the sun, somewhere
Not even comets live.

WHEN KAYLI IS HERSELF

A warm hand rests on my shoulder
And for an ecstatic moment I think
I left the mudroom door unlocked
And Samir has silently crawled in

With me

But it's not Samir, the thin wrist wears
A hospital bracelet and has pink painted nails.
Kayli's long lashes rest on shining cheeks
It's hot up here, she says without opening

Her eyes

I slip my arms around her and squeeze
Until she calls me *an incestuous lesbian*
But she squeezes back, smelling rank
And medicinal. She's sweaty too—we both

Are

I wouldn't believe the sun rose again
The world kept turning and orbiting
As though today was just another day but
Above the open skylight the sky is glowing

Blue

Like nothing dreadful happened last night
Wheezing, Kayli leans back and thoughtfully
Considers the state of my unplucked eyebrows
Where's Samir? is just the first of her

Questions.

SISTERLY ADVICE

You should tell Mom
Is what Kayli says
After I have confessed
Almost everything
About Samir and David.

(I don't mention the car wash.
She can't know about that.
The official story is still that it was "great fun.")

Poor David
She says about Michael
Were you sleeping with him too?
I shake my head and suffer
As Kayli's questions get
More and more
Indiscreet.
She always could
Make me reveal anything
She wants to know
Everything.

I spew out monotone
Salacious details
And sad ones
While she listens
Entranced.

I keep talking
I don't want to stop
I want her to listen
Forever
To never leave this room
To never leave me
Because she is
My best friend
Maybe the only friend
I have left.

NEWSFLASH

What happened with Parker?
I ask when I run out of my own tragedy
He mutated, Kayli says
And I wait for the rest of the story.

Don't tell Mom, okay?
We made this plan to sneak away
And, you know, do it
But I changed my mind

And he got all pissy.
Then he said I was a slut
Which is, HELLO, illogical
But everyone believed it.

What an asshole!
I thought he was supposed to be a Christian
Newsflash, Rah Rah
Christians can be douchebags.

And she stares at my slanted ceiling
Tears dripping into her ears
Reminding me
She's human too.

LIFE GOES ON

Marika barely waits for her mother to leave
Before typing quickly

What

Is

W r o n g?

David's brother died of an overdose, I say
And she doesn't even spell out
A strong specific word
She just hits a button

Bad

Bad

Bad

And then

Sorry.

What

Happened?

And so I
Tell her the whole
Sordid story too
Like I can't keep the words inside
How I used them both
And betrayed them
For no good reason.
She falls silent
Not her good silence
But a reproachful
Judgmental one
And we spend the day like that
Me wondering
If I've lost her too.

TEXTS TO SAMIR

Talk to me.

Forgive me.

My mind isn't right. I AM crazy.

I love you. Please answer me.

I didn't mean to hurt anyone. I lost control of my life.

I'm so sorry.

Until finally Marika grabs my phone from my hand.
She's surprisingly fast at texting.

*This is Marika. Ella has been crying all day. It's getting
annoying. Pls reply.*

To which Samir texts back:

Will call 2night. Late.

ON THE OTHER HAND

All texts to David
Are revised, then deleted
And nothing is sent.

EPIC

Marika bends her head
Over her iPad typing
Ignoring me
My feet get numb
In the kiddy pool
Marika made it clear

I

Don't

Want

To

Swim

Which is how I know
She's really mad at me
Normally she loves it.

Marika types
And children stare
And fretful mothers
Pull them away
Shielding them
From their own rudeness
As though it's a disease.

Marika frowns with concentration
Her tanned fingers thrumming
And I suspect her composition
Might be aimed at me.

MARIKA'S WISDOM

I used to throw tantrums

When I was little

It was torture

Learning to speak

And Mom would say:

"You have to name your pain."

Name your pain, Ella.

Mom would say:

"It's easier to run from a lion

Than some shadow in the dark."

I'm not mad at you.

If you can't talk to me,

Talk to someone.

Please.

CROSSHAIRS

Now I feel like
I am walking around
With rifle crosshairs
On the entire world

Well maybe not a rifle
It's not that I want
To shoot someone
Apart from myself
Occasionally

Only now I look at Mom
And Kayli painting her toenails
Ms. Sagal and Dad
And ask myself
Is this the person I can talk to?
But I have an excuse for each of them
I have caused them enough pain
Or they have their own problems
Or maybe I'm scared of
How bad I would feel
If they can't hide the fact
That they don't really care.

PENCIL

It's painstaking work
Carefully rendering
In lethally sharp pencil
Every detail
Of Marika's speech app
With her gnarled hand
Curled finger pressing on the word
BAD.

In the corner
Barely visible
A tendril of black
Lace.

EGGS AND OTHER ROUND OBJECTS

To my surprise
Sarah emails

We're going to Michael's funeral
Mom thought you might like to come
I know how weird it can be
In an unfamiliar place
I was freaking out at Genie's mom's funeral
All those creepy flowers.

Have you spoken to David?
He won't answer his phone
Or return my texts
I guess we'll see him there
I hope he's okay

The service is at six tomorrow
We'll pick you up at five
After we can go to his house
And do the shiva thing
Mom can explain it

I'll grab you something on the way
From the kosher deli, egg salad
Or bagels, something round
Did you know Michael very well?
I went to his bar mitzvah.

What a messed-up world.

THE END

Samir calls
As promised
Close to midnight.

We cry
And he says
I can't do this anymore.

He adds
We can't stay
Friends. That's bullshit.

You
Are not
A good friend.

My heart is
Torn in pieces
My soul is corrupted

You
Did this
You ruined me.

I listen
To his rage
His heartbreak and

I do
Not dare
To disagree.

MIDNIGHT

As quietly as I can
I slip my bicycle
Out the garage side door.

No helmet
The night wind blows
My wrinkled cotton dress
Around my knees
I stay on the sidewalk
For safety. I want to arrive
At my destination alive
The address from research papers
In Dad's study.

Ella?
Kieran says
What are you doing here?
Wanna go for a walk?
I say
We tuck my bike
In his hallway
And head out
Into the dark.

Kieran lights a joint
And we pass it back and forth
As we walk around the lake
Better?

He says
Flicking the butt into the water.

You seemed a little tense before
I heard about your boyfriend's brother
That's too bad.

He's not my boyfriend
I say
Yeah, says Kieran
Does he know that?

WHAT DOES HE KNOW?

All I've ever done is toy with David
Like a cat with a crippled mouse.

All I've done is evade questions
I've avoided moments where
Feelings are discussed
Focused on other things
Myself mainly
My anxieties
My stupid plan
My selfishness.

My shame
Makes me stumble
I sit on the curb.
Whoa, are you okay?
Kieran asks
Not really, I say.

I search his face
Hoping maybe he's the one
Who will listen to the whole
Sad and sorry tale
And tell me what to do
But undergrad degree or no
He's just a stoned boy
Looking down my dress
And I don't even like him.

Though I let him kiss me
Later in his front hall
His smoky sour tongue
Flops in my mouth
Like a rancid fish
I'd gag if I could be bothered.

And when I put a stop to it
He holds the door
While I push my bicycle out
And doesn't say, "I'll call you"
Or any other platitude
For that anyway
I'm grateful.
And more I suppose
Because he's shown me
Something important
About me
That I didn't know I knew.

This:
At least I don't hate myself enough
To have sex with a guy like him.

INVISIBLE

The on-ramp is quiet
But for occasional trucks
Rumbling like distant thunder

The gas station emits
Weak and sickly
Zombie light

I lock my bike
And turn down into the dark
Staring at the spot

The hidey-hole between
Two Dumpsters wondering
What magnet held me there

I would like to shake that girl
And ask her why it matters
Why she cared so much

She waited in the dark
For something to happen
Almost as if she wanted it

To be broken down beaten
Left for dead but no one even
Noticed she was there.

MOONLIGHT

By the time
I reach the deep scrub
My bare legs feel flayed.
I'd raise my head
And howl at the moon
But I don't need to.

She appears
Damp fur and coiled muscles
Ready to flee
To leap back into her dark
Primitive past.

I would like to think
She was drawn by our moonlight bond
But it's more likely the hotdog
I've placed on the ground between us.

I've been thinking about you, I say
She snuffles as she gobbles my gift.
Ignoring me
I swear I think
She even rolls her eyes.

How do you tolerate all this?
I ask, looking around
At the highway, the on-ramp
The gas station

The Dumpsters
The truckers, the taxi drivers
Unbuckling.

How do you stay you?
How do you not lie down
On the road and let a truck
Crush the wild out of you?

Surely you of all creatures
Must be weighed down
By the hypocrisy
The betrayal of a God
Who gave you a perfect world
Then populated it with
Imperfection
Personified
Who plowed and
Paved your
Paradise.

She licks ketchup from her maw
Yellow teeth, pink gums
And stares back
Low growling
All coyote, she has
Nothing to say to my
Irrelevance

But her tail disappearing
In the long grass.

Tell me what to do!
I call after her
At first only the cool
Night wind
Replies.

But then
From the dark
She howls
Twice as though
Begrudgingly
She's giving me
Her best advice.

TORN

The synagogue is packed
Sarah and I stand at the back.

Apparently David has hardly said a word
To anyone since it happened,
Sarah whispers
As the rabbi says things in Hebrew
And English things that are meant
To console.

In the front row David
Towers above his mother
Even with slumped shoulders
His head hanging down.

His lawyer father
Stands gray wool and stiff
On the other side.
No one for him to
Prosecute here but God
And I'm surprised to find
I can forgive him for
The near ruination he inflicted
On me and Samir last year
I wonder if this is God's punishment
For his self-serving hubris.

The thought makes my heart
Flicker like a faulty light
One of those ones that
Makes the whole string fail
If God was meting judgment
I wonder
What would he have in store
For me?

BROKEN BOY: PART ONE

He bounces a basketball
His tie loosened
Torn shirt untucked
As mourners trail into his house

He doesn't shoot for the hoop
Or respond to people
Who try to say hello
He bounces a basketball

Like the beating of a heart
One-handed, rhythmic
One player short for one-on-one
He doesn't shoot for the hoop

That effort would require
Raising his head to see
The front door open and close
Like the beating of a heart

He sees me and drops the ball
As he disappears inside
He doesn't speak, lacking the will
That effort would require.

WHAT I DESERVE

So you're the shiksa
An ancient woman says to me.
Bubbe! someone says
In a scandalized tone
But the old lady is unchastened.
I'm Ella, I say
I'm a friend of David's.
A little more than a friend
To hear him tell it
Bubbe says with a sniff.
Men hide from pain
Like dying cats.
See if you can get him
To come out of his room.

BROKEN BOY: PART TWO

But I'm smart enough to know
David won't be in his room
I find him on Michael's bed
Where we laid him that day
Surrounded by towels
And watched him
Made hopeful by his promise
Not knowing what it meant.
That WAS the last time.

He doesn't look at me
Just stares at the ceiling
I heard you haven't been talking
I try a peace offering
I guess I can't blame you
For not wanting to talk to me.

And he doesn't
He just slides to one side
Inviting me to lie next to him
I move slowly
Take off your shoes, he snaps
I do and anticipate
Him enumerating what else
He wants me to take off
Which I would do
Right now I would peel
Off layers until there was nothing

Left of me but bones
A grinning skull on the pillow
Next to him.

I won't share you with Samir
He says while I try to conceal
The minor freak-out I'm having
At the idea that this is even up
For discussion.

We broke up, I say
For good this time?
For good, for bad
Forever.
That's over.

DAVID SPEAKS HIS MIND

I'm not a very assertive guy
But I'm going to try
This next year is going to be awful
I can't screw up grade twelve
I want to get into a good school
For architecture
And I think it might be easier
With someone to…like…
Cheer me on.
I know you're probably
Not the best person for that role
But the amount of bullshit
I would have to deal with
To find someone else is not worth it.

Wow, I don't know what to say
I'm overwhelmed by your offer
It's so romanti—

Shut up.
On any other day
I'd be telling you
I never want to see you again
But I haven't slept in days
I'm exhausted, my throat
Feels raw from sobbing
Like a two-year-old
And right now all I want
To do is spoon you.

I roll onto my side
Obediently
And he curls into my back
My head tucked into his shoulder.

If this is love
He says into my hair
It really sucks.

MAYBE WE WILL MAKE IT

Because I listen to him cry quietly
For a few minutes before he moves back
Rolling me over to face him and
After I wipe away his tears he leans in and
Whispers something very naughty in my ear.

But later, he says
In a few weeks maybe
I'm too messed up right now
I think I would break into a million pieces.
Also, I don't want to be that guy
Who is always begging for it
So if you don't want to that's fine
But you should tell me now.

I take a moment to process that
It seems a little clinical
Like washy wishy
Soft and squishy David
Has been replaced
By a more officious twin.

You won't have to beg, I say.
Then he lets me kiss him
Like I've wanted to for months
Nothing tentative this time
About his lips and tongue
He slides my thigh

Over his hip and moves
One hand over my breast
Giving it an emphatic squeeze
Like a promise
His eyes close and that's how
Holding on to my boob
Wrapped up in me
He drifts off to sleep.

As the day fades to night
Bubbe appears
A stout silhouette
Against the hall light
Humph, she says
And closes the door.

chapter eleven

INFINITE

HIATUS

David says
We should have some time
Apart
He needs to work on forgiving me
But right now
He's busy
Forgiving Michael.

You need to forgive me too, he says
For what? I almost say
But my throat burns
Tied in a knot with the anger
I still hold for him
The night in jail
The lawyer and
Panic, how I
Drowned in
Panic
That pours out of me
As tears.

See? I knew it, he says
You wouldn't behave like that
Without a reason.

We hold each other
The words
I'm so sorry
Orbiting us and then
We give each other space
And time
Which after all
Are both
Infinite.

TEXTILE COLLAGE

I shred old jeans
A once-white towel
Now gray
A tattered pair of mittens
And snip and glue
Shaping, fluffing
Until a coyote's paw
Pads quietly among
The oppressive hands.

A coyote's paw
Is for standing
For grounding
I wonder, if we walked
On our hands
As animals do
Would the world feel more like
Something that supports us
Instead of something
We have to hold up?

BUSTED

Raphaelle!
Dad shouts up my stairs
Along with my middle name
AND last name
That's how I know
I'm in big trouble.

I had an interesting conversation
With one of my students
He begins
Oh shit, I think.
And he yells at me
For ten minutes
About smoking pot
With Kieran
And Mom joins us
And shares the news
That she found
A condom wrapper
Under my bed
And I'm about to get
So grounded I'll practically be
Dead and buried.
And Dad says
Jesus Christ
Did you sleep with Kieran?!
And I say
No, I did not sleep with Kieran

It was Samir
Only Samir
But we broke up
So you don't have to worry
About that anymore.
But they both keep yelling
Until even Kayli is telling them
Stop it! Stop it!
Can't you see how upset she is?
And everyone stops
And sees.

TEARS

For my little meltdown
I get:
A hug from Kayli
A glass of water from Dad
And an interrogation from Mom.
Was that a panic attack?
I used to get them too
All through high school.
I would wake up
Unable to breathe.
Is it like that?
Are you eating?
You look thin
Are you throwing up?
Are you sleeping?
Do you want to try pills again?
And Dad
Who prefers an unmedicated life
Says, *Maybe she could share a room*
With Kayli again
She might sleep better.
And when Kayli hears this
Despite her earlier support
She screams until
She has an asthma attack
I've got to give it to her
She knows how to work a crowd.
So Dad says

My house, my rules
Stop being so selfish
Then Kayli says
Can't she just find another boy
To keep her company?
And Dad says
Watch your mouth, young lady
Which makes her go crazy
Wheezing and screeching
So even though I'm grounded
And under observation
I just walk out.
I figure I'm seventeen
That's old enough
To join the army
Right?

HEAT STROKE

No sunscreen
No sunglasses
No hat
Bare shoulders
All I have
Is a bus pass
Phone
Flip-flops
And five bucks
In the pocket of
My overalls.

I buy a Gatorade
And park my butt
Under a tree
By the lake
Thinking
I should have
Spent the whole
Summer here
Watching ducks.
And I mean
The WHOLE summer
Day and night
Twenty-four/seven.

DEADLY SERIOUS

As the air finally cools
My phone beeps
Samir:

I need to talk to you
Tonight
Can you meet me?

He gives an intersection
When I reach it
I realize it's his mosque.

Samir stands
Rather formally dressed
Between the columns.

When I join him I see
His parents and sister
Standing nearby.

Samir turns to look at them
A beseeching look on his face
His father's eyes narrow
And I begin to suspect
Some kind of intervention.

Look, I know this is—
Samir begins
But his father clears his throat
Rather forcefully.

And Samir snaps
Something back in Arabic
Obviously his father
Is unmoved.

Poor Samir
He's still very cute
When he sulks.
Until he sighs
And says
Raphaelle, will you marry me?

COOL

And it takes all my
Self-control to breathe through the
Urge to laugh out loud.

PARENTS OF THE YEAR

But it goes on
Samir crosses his arms
And looks anywhere but at me.

You will have to convert
Samir says
But, well, will you?
He recites tonelessly
Like a bad actor
Will-you-convert-to-Islam-and-marry-me?

By now I have an idea
Of what's going on
And I play along
Because poor Samir
Is as red as the setting sun.

No, I say.
I don't think that's a good idea.
Samir turns to his family
Happy?

How do you feel?
His mother says
And Samir answers
With a stream of Arabic
That makes his sister hide her smile.
In English, his father says.

Embarrassed, Samir says
Humiliated.

And?

And ashamed.
I feel
Ashamed.

His father looks satisfied
We'll see you inside, he says.

RELIEVED

Would you have married me
If I'd said yes?
I suppose, Samir says to his feet.

You shouldn't feel ashamed
We didn't do anything wrong
We were careful, mostly
And we love each other
We loved each other
How can that be wrong?

If you fall in love
With another Muslim
Or any pious man
He might not want you
Because you're not a virgin.

I'll have to make sure
That doesn't happen then
No more pious men for me
Anyway, you're not
A virgin either.

It doesn't work that way
He says, and I can almost taste
His bitterness
A Muslim girl only wants
To be respected

But now I'll always want
What you let me have.

He turns his head away
So fast I wonder
For a moment
If I've slapped him
Or if he only expects me to
For showing me a side of him
He usually hides so well.

That's a revolting thing to say
I tell him, measuring my voice
Like strong medicine
Don't ever say that
To me or to any girl
Ever again
For any reason.

Samir falls silent
Still as the marble columns
And I'm tempted
To stomp away
End it with an exclamation mark
But I can see that he is crying.

Habibi, I say
Gently.

Don't call me that, he says
Wiping his eyes
I don't think you will ever be able
To see the world as I do.
I need to go pray.

As he turns I call after him
Samir!
You should tell your parents
About Ashraf's wedding
They have a right to know.

He slips off his shoes at the door
Without looking back
And says, *Maybe I will.*

MYSTERIOUS WAYS: PART ONE

The steps of the mosque
Are cool stone
And feel ancient
As I sit and watch
The dark curtain of night
Rise around me.

The chanting song from inside
Washes over me
Like clear water
And I hear the end
Of summer humming
Somewhere too
Just beyond my reach.

MYSTERIOUS WAYS: PART TWO

An old man sits down next to me
Do you have questions about Islam?
No, I say quickly
I'm just resting.

Rest is good, he says
I guess he must be some kind of priest
And he's a good one
Because his quiet company eats at me
Until I can't help but speak.

What does Islam say about someone
Who can't seem to stop
Doing stupid, thoughtless things?
Who can't stop thinking
About stuff that scares her?
Who keeps getting betrayed
By people she should know
Better than to trust?
Who might be hurting herself
Without even realizing?

The man turns to me
Islam would say
That person is probably a teenager
Then he gives me a cheeky smile
Or perhaps you are possessed by Djinn
Gin, I say. Like the drink?

Djinn, he says
Mischievous spirits.
The English word is—

I interrupt
I know, I say

The English word is *Genie.*

I can't help it
I start to giggle.

THE SIDEWALK LESS TRAVELED

There are two ways back to my house
I could skirt the park and cross the footbridge by
The mansions with their water-sucking lawns
Grab the express bus to the coffee shop
And take a short walk up our street.

Or I could board the winding bus
And take a tour of familiar places
School, the spot where Samir and I ate baklava
And the ballpark where I howled at the moon
What difference would it make?

I choose the first way, the walk
Will do me good, the fresh night air
The quiet streets, excited crickets
Though the other route, to be honest
Probably involves as much walking.

One day I might look back and wonder
Why I took this way tonight of all nights
I could have done my usual meandering
Instead, I point myself like a ship's prow
And make landfall in front of Genie's house.

IN GENIE'S FRONT YARD

What are YOU doing here?
Go away.

You're still here.
What is the matter with you?

You have to leave.
My dad is getting suspicious.

Freakazoid!
Get lost!

You can't just stand in our yard all night!
What do you want?

I have nothing to say to her, Dad!
I have nothing to say to you.

Please, Ella, Dad's asking questions now.
I'll get grounded again.

I'm sorry, okay?
Now go.

You're crazy!
Why are you doing this to me?

INSIDE OUT

I had an epiphany
I say
Genie sighs, sits
And pulls out her phone

epiphany *[i-'pi-fǝ-nē] n pl -nies*
a sudden, intuitive perception of or insight into reality or
the essential meaning of something, often initiated by some
simple, commonplace occurrence.

Go on, she says

It happened on the steps of the mosque
Samir and I had one of those final scenes
I'll tell you about it one day
It was crushing, but kind of priceless

Anyway, after I was just sitting there
And this old dude started talking to me
He might have been some kind of priest
Long story why, but I thought of you.

And I saw you then, but inside out
And I saw things I recognized
And it terrified me to think that maybe
Everybody looks like that on the inside.

I know now that Samir does, and David
And Kayli, my mom, my dad even
Marika, Sarah, Kieran, it's getting so
I don't want to look into people anymore.

Somehow I thought you might be
The one who was neat and tidy inside,
I thought your meanness required control
But maybe you're just as random as the rest of us.

I take things too personally
It felt like you wanted me dead
But now I'm starting to think
It was never about me, was it?

BLUE BALLPOINT

Do you have a pen and paper?
I ask
I want to draw your hand.

You're so weird, Genie says
But she goes inside
And comes back out
With paper and a blue ballpoint.

I hate blue ink
So it seems fitting
But soon I'm frustrated
Freckles are hard to draw, I say.
Try living with them, she says.
And then
Want to hear all the names
I've been called?

Spot, spotty, leopard
Leper, patch, pixels
Spackle, speckle
Freckle-face
Pox, poxy
Measles, dotty
Speck, splatter
Sprinkles, fly poop.

She sighs.
Ugly, fat, stupid.

I reach forward
And take her hand
Turning it over.
Palms are easier anyway, I say.

And let my fingers
Linger
On her wrist
On
A
Thin
White
Scar.

STARS

Genie falls back
Like she's been shot
In a movie
Slow motion.
Her head rests in
The long grass.
She stares up
While the last glow of day
Leaves the sky.

I watch her
And wait
Expecting
Something
Crucial.

I don't speak
But for the scratching
Of the blue pen
Tracing her life line
Her love line
Her fingerprints.
If there's one thing
Marika has taught me
It is the value
Of silence.

UNDERNEATH

Do you know how breast cancer kills?
It's not the cancer in the breast.
That doesn't matter.
It gets into other things.
The lungs. The liver.
My mother's brain.
In the end she didn't know who I was.
I'd tell her that I love her.
"What?" she'd say.
Once she said,
"Where's my daughter?"

I've never told anyone this before
This is not an excuse.
Reasons aren't excuses.
Samir broke my heart.
Sarah was my best friend.
You have everything.

It wasn't my idea to leave you.
It was one of those other bitches
But she was just trying to impress me
As if that will make a difference
In her pathetic life.
I hate those girls.
I hate all girls.
Especially myself.

Our parents look at us and wonder
Why we are the way we are
The moods and tears
The bullying, the jealousy.
But what do they expect?
Surrounded by rivals all the time
Like jackals fighting for a bone
Failure shoved in your face
Teachers looking at us
Like we're shit on their shoes.
They've forgotten what it feels like.
Maybe we will forget one day too.
I sure hope so.

I heard your mom had bulimia.
Of all the things to be jealous of.
That's fucked up.
I want a mom with your mom's disease
Instead of the one I had and lost.

MY OFFERING

I join her
Lying back on the grass
Looking up through the branches
To the drifting silver clouds
The black sky above that
And beyond
The ozone layer
The orbit of the moon
The sun and planets
The Oort cloud, the heliopause
Space, the galaxy
Nebula, stars
The entire universe
And everything beyond
And everyone
Who has ever lived and died
Every atom of them
Goes on somewhere.
As beautiful as that seems
It is also terrifying
So precarious
A delicate balancing act
A fragile house of cards
An infinitely complex machine
That can never be understood.
No wonder I hide inside myself.

I cried, I tell Genie
The day I learned

How big the moon really was
And that it didn't float
Around our sky
Like a lost balloon.

I used to let balloons go
On purpose, she replies
And pray for them to come back
How stupid is that?
Like God would care
About a balloon.
Like there even is a God.
Like he helped
The football team
Win the regionals
But ignored me
Begging him
BEGGING him
To let Mom live.
What an asshole.

A swarm of bats flies
Across the moonlit
Silver sky
Gross, Genie says
And somewhere
So far away in time and space
That maybe only I can hear
The coyote howls.

INVERSION

I lock the mudroom door
Behind me
Because my mind and me
Need some time alone.

Pulling all the hands down from the wall
I lay them on the bed
Then, starting with the coyote paw
I grow a tree of hands
Back on the wall

The wild furry paw
Part of a sturdy trunk.
I flip the hands upward
The fingers bent or straight
Curled, waving, pointing
But not at me anymore
Not pushing down
Grasping
But branches
Lifting
Growing
Into the open
Sky.

Genie's hand tucks in
Like all the others.
There's nothing special
Or magical

Or dangerous about it.
It's just a hand
With a scar more visible
Than anyone else's.

I throw away my own hand.
The dripping sponge doesn't fit
Somehow
It's like a storm cloud
In a blue sky.

Instead
I coat my hand in red lipstick
I never wear it
And press a print right on the wall.
At the top
Perched there
Like a vibrant tropical bird
Poised to fly
Away.

TRUST

Then I make a secret plan
A vow for grade twelve
I will become Genie's best friend.
What could be more audacious than that?

Maybe together we could use our powers
For good instead of chaos and heartbreak.
I'm probably an idiot.
She's screwed me over twice now.

But there's something about the idea
Of friendship with Genie that intrigues me.
Like the wild, wiry coyote
The vibrant bird and me maybe

She lurks on the fringes of civilization
Waiting for someone to tame her
And after all, if I can make a coyote sing
Maybe
      I
          Can
               Do
                    Anything.

ACKNOWLEDGMENTS

Sometimes I think editing a book must be like psycho-analyzing someone. If this is true, then Sarah Harvey knows me better than almost anyone in the world. Without her gentleness and rigorousness, this book would never have been finished. Thanks go to her and everyone at Orca for being so fabulous. Thank you Aida Bardissi for invaluable help with Arabic language and culture. Thanks to Kris and Carolyn at the Carolyn Swayze Literary Agency for making it possible to complete (continue?) Ella's story.

To my patient husband and tolerant daughter—I know it's not easy to live with a writer in the house. Thank you for understanding. Mum and my beautiful sisters—I could not do this without your unconditional love.

GABRIELLE PRENDERGAST

is a UK-born Canadian/Australian who lives in Vancouver, British Columbia, with her husband and daughter. She holds an MFA in Creative Writing from the University of British Columbia. A part-time teacher and mentor, Gabrielle is the author of the verse novel *Audacious* (the first book featuring Ella), which was shortlisted for a CLA Award.

She can be found online at www.angelhorn.com and www.versenovels.com.

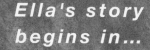

Ella's story
begins in...

AUDACIOUS

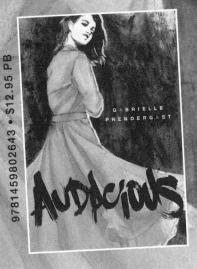

9781459802643 • $12.95 PB

Nothing is simple for Ella. Not
family. Not friends. Not school.
And especially not romance. Ella
can't do anything right, except
draw. But even her art is wrong—
and more dangerous than she
could have imagined.

*"Fans of Ellen Hopkins and Sonya Sones's novels in verse will
delight in Prendergast's rich, riveting story...Prendergast
demonstrates a powerful understanding of the adolescent search
for identity, and her writing uses the verse format to great effect."*
—PUBLISHERS WEEKLY

 ORCA BOOK PUBLISHERS
www.orcabook.com • 1-800-210-5277